Blood
Moon

Ellen Parry Lewis

Metal Lunchbox Publishing

Text copyright 2017 by Ellen Parry Lewis
Cover Design and Illustration copyright 2017 by SF Varney

ISBN: 978-0-9843437-4-4

DEDICATION

For *Estellise*

ACKNOWLEDGMENTS

As always, I'd like to thank the Creator of the heavens and the earth. I pray before I begin any writing because without Him, I'm nothing. I'd also like to thank Sam Varney of Metal Lunchbox Publishing for his unfailing enthusiasm and commitment to my projects. Thanks to my husband Al for not only his encouragement, but for being my unofficial editor. I love you.

Additionally, thanks to my friend Emily for being another one of my unofficial editors; your constant texts and even illustrations were a big help. My daughter, Estellise--you had no idea, but playing with you is what gave me this idea, so thanks for the inspiration and for the fun, super imaginative playtimes. And thanks to Otis for giving me the time to write. To my family and friends--thank you for your love and support!

Prologue

I remember the feeling of the fine sand on the beach, sliding pleasantly between my toes. The sun was bright, and I was thankful to walk on dry land after more than a week bobbing on the sea.

Directly past the beach was something even more spectacular than the bright white sand, though.

"What is it?" I turned and asked my father who had walked up behind me.

"I'm guessing it's the Gate of Wrotins, but it looks more like a wall," he replied, his eyes squinting at the tower structure before us, bathed in shadows as the sun was just slightly behind it from our position.

I was small at the time, only six years old, so I couldn't accurately determine how tall the structure really was. However, I did tell my father, "It must be a hundred times my height!"

He had laughed only slightly at that and responded, "Almost, dear." He turned then and backtracked toward the ship where my mother and her best friend, Mrs. Lindle, had just disembarked.

I turned back to face the impressive structure before me, but I could clearly hear Mrs. Lindle's obnoxious exclamations of relief. "I couldn't have stayed even one more hour on that boat!"

I tried my best to ignore her as I continued to stare at the wall. It appeared to be made entirely of gray stone, though it was difficult to see at parts due to the thick leafy vines that covered it. The wall stretched perhaps a minute's walk in each direction, though walking around it might be difficult, as the vines seemed to have overtaken the entire island, covering the trees like long snakes.

"Sarah!" It was my mother's voice. I ran back to where she was still standing on the edge of the beach with Mrs. Lindle, my father no longer in sight.

"Wait here with us. Father and Mr. Abble have just gone below deck to find some things to use to clear the vines."

I nodded happily, and my mother threw me a kind smile as Mrs. Lindle continued her rant as if there had been no interruption. "When you said it was going to be more than a week, I never dreamed how draining the constant motion of the waves would be. It feels like I'm still bouncing around, even on this sand!"

It was obvious to me that my mother was not entirely listening to Mrs. Lindle, for her eyes kept wandering to the wall, surveying it discreetly. I often wondered why my mother was friends with Mrs. Lindle, the two being different in every way so far as I could tell. Mrs. Lindle was loud, always with a breath-stealing corset on her curvy body and her brown hair up in the tightest of buns. My mother, on the other hand, was a patient, soft-spoken woman. She lacked almost any curves and stood noticeably tall. Her looser, often flowing dresses were never tied too tightly around her thin body, and she always wore her bright blonde hair in a casually tied braid. Her blue eyes, just a shade lighter than my own, smiled delicately, and her hands and thin fingers danced gracefully as she talked.

One time I had actually asked my mother why she was friends with Mrs. Lindle. My mother had laughed lightly and replied, "I can't give you a specific reason. I suppose opposites attract."

That logic seemed true when it came to my mother's marriage to my father, though quite unlike my feelings toward Mrs. Lindle, I absolutely adored my father. My father was almost a foot shorter than my mother, an almost laughable difference when they stood together. He always wore round, thick glasses, and his mop of brown hair was consistently disheveled. He was loud and talkative, but in an endearing way, as he easily grew excited by things. Though it was partly from his energetic excitement that we found ourselves on that specific island that day.

"Here we are! Machetes!" Father exclaimed as he reappeared from below deck, the sharp weapon in his hand. Mr. Abble, the owner of the boat and hired help for the expedition, came up behind Father, holding his own machete.

"What do you say we go find this treasure?" Father nearly shouted enthusiastically, and he marched toward the great wall, the rest of us at his heels.

Reaching the shade of the intimidating structure, the sand felt cold beneath my bare feet. I shivered even though the air was still warm; something about this place set the tiny blonde hairs on my arms straight up as my skin tingled uncomfortably.

"All right. Let's take a look at the map, shall we?" Father said, pulling the wrinkled piece of browning paper from his pocket. He and my mother had found it behind a framed painting amongst my mother's older belongings the month before. Though the paper looked plenty old enough to me, my father said it was probably much older than it looked, the paper having been protected from tearing or disintegrating by some sort of protection spell. I had looked at it casually upon its discovery, but it hadn't made much sense to me. A lot of ancient script and some poorly drawn buildings, but my father and mother had quickly come to the conclusion that it was a map marking a specific destination at this island. I never bothered to ask the specifics, only gathering that we would be going on a grand adventure to find a treasure—at least that's what my father thought. My mother didn't seem as certain that we would find gold and jewels, though she was still plenty curious. And so after my mother extended her invitation to Mrs. Lindle to accompany us, with Mrs. Lindle leaving her four-year-old daughter in the hands of her much more subdued husband for the duration of the voyage, we went to procure a boat.

The time on the boat had been boring, though certainly not as tortuous as Mrs. Lindle had made it sound, and I was ready to explore and dig for buried treasure.

"So, the writing here says that one of us has to touch the stone in the center and the gate will open," my father was saying as I continued staring at the wall before me. To my side, Father and Mr. Abble started cutting away at the vines, trying to find a door, I supposed. I knew my mother or I would have to be the ones to touch the door; my father had already deciphered the language to read "the handprint of an immortal." To the best of my knowledge, my mother and I were the only two in our little party who fit that description. Still, immortals were generally feared and mistrusted, and so we never spoke of this, even to Mrs. Lindle. As I was still so young, I didn't quite understand it, except that my parents warned me to never discuss it with anyone. I knew that one day, when it was apparent that my mother was not aging at all, we would be forced to leave and find a new place to live so that no one would notice, but I never really

5

thought about that day as it seemed so distant to me.

Several minutes passed, and my father and Mr. Abble still had not discovered the door. I grew impatient, and reached out my hand to touch the wall through the vines. Nothing happened, so I walked in the opposite direction of my father, finding the wall move loudly and abruptly under my touch perhaps only ten seconds later. "I found something!" I yelled, giddy with excitement as the adults rushed over to me. A doorway had indeed opened through the wall, snapping the vines around it as it seemingly melted out of the way.

I ran through first, my own flowing summer dress catching playfully on the vines at the edge of the perfectly maintained dark dirt path.

"I know that this island used to belong to the Hersotes, but I never imagined that their magic would stay this long. Look at this path! It doesn't have a single thing growing on it to block it up!" Mrs. Lindle exclaimed.

"It is extraordinary," Father agreed, bending down and feeling the soft dirt with his hands.

I was much more excited by the flowers growing along the edge of the path, brilliant red and the size of my torso! It looked like they grew even closer together further along, and so I began to skip ahead, my undone, long, bright blonde hair flying behind me.

"Don't stray too far!" my mother called after me.

"All right!" I called back, stopping here or there to smell an oversized flower. I could hear the adults walking behind me, making slow progress as they kept stopping to examine and admire various plants.

Only a couple of minutes down the path, the ground rose up at a steep incline, and so I focused on my steps. In only a few minutes though, I was at the top of a large hill where the terrain flattened out once more. I continued happily skipping down the path until I stopped abruptly a minute later when I spied a simple but large structure before me.

There were nine pillars creating a ring, each standing tall behind a gray stone throne. There was grass in this area, bright green and plush, though close to the ground. Impulsively, I jumped up into the throne closest to me. I glanced at the surrounding chairs, wondering what sort of a place this had been when the other immortals had lived here. Looking down then, I noticed a flat stone with symbols on it sitting in the grass. It was only perhaps half a foot in diameter. Glancing around, it looked like each throne had one before it. And so, with the innocence of my age, I hopped down and on top of it. Each was too far to hop between without touching the grass, but that didn't stop me from trying. Three big hops and I was on the next one. Three more hops to the next one, but the moment I touched it, some force sent me flying several feet from it, as if it were on a spring. It felt strange to be sure, but as I wasn't hurt, I stood and brushed off my dress, though there were only grass stains on it. Deciding to avoid that one, I moved to hop to the next one.

The second my feet hit the next smooth, flat stone, the sky went dark. My breath caught in my throat. For a moment, I panicked thinking that my eyes had suddenly failed me. But then the dark silhouettes of trees came into focus around the throne clearing. Staring straight above me then, I saw stars, thousands of them, and a bright full moon. I had only been looking at the beautiful sky above me for a few seconds when the moon fell dark only to be quickly replaced with a moon of all red. I had never seen anything like it before. It was oddly beautiful.

I was about to call for my parents when I jumped at the sound of an unrecognizable female voice coming at me from seemingly all sides:

Blood of mine
Life of blood
It drips to you
Mistakes undone
Call the power of your blood
Send to every corner
Death for those who wait forever

As the haunting voice began to speak those same words over again, I noticed movement on the moon above me, amidst the ever-twinkling white stars. The red began dripping toward the bottom of the moon, revealing white underneath, as if the moon were melting.

"Sarah!" I heard a voice call through the dark.

"Mother!" I cried back desperately, by now quite fearful in this eerie blackness beneath the melting moon. I looked in the direction I knew the path to be, searching in vain for my mother when the red from the moon fell brightly from above my head, around the corner where I had been looking, and out of sight past the dark trees.

"Mother!" I shouted again, leaping in the direction of the red. The second my feet hit the soft grass again, I shielded my eyes, for the sun was once more bright.

But as soon as I covered my eyes, I heard my father shout my mother's name in panic, "Florence!"

"Mother!" I cried out again, running back to the path. The second I rounded the corner I saw my father slouched on the ground, cradling my mother's limp body. There was what appeared to be spatters of blood on her off-white dress, though in only a second, they seemed to soak into her dress and disappear completely. Mrs. Lindle was crouched down next to her too, whispering her name frantically into her ear while Mr. Abble remained standing, staring suspiciously around in all directions.

"Florence! Speak to me," my father was imploring her urgently.

Mrs. Lindle grabbed her wrist. "She has no pulse," she said after a while.

My feet remained glued to the ground, looking on in panic.

"She has to have a pulse. She can't die," my father said urgently. "Florence! Are you all right?" My father began crying as he wiped some loose strands of hair from my mother's face.

"She can't be dead," I croaked.

My father looked up at me, relief crossing his face for a moment as he saw me. "Mrs. Lindle, take Sarah back to the boat immediately," my father said. Mrs. Lindle stood at once and gently picked me up, hurrying back down the hill with me in her arms, hiding my face against her shoulder.

Confusion clouded my sadness. My mother was an immortal, a Hersote. She couldn't die.

But she had. And I feared that I was to blame. It had been an accident, of course, but I had been the one to send the moon's blood to kill her.

Chapter One

Celia was singing a high, soft melody that bounced playfully on the breeze. My long, dirty blonde hair tried to fly into the air with that same breeze, seemingly dancing along with it even though I was reclined peacefully with my knees bent. Raela joined in with her twin sister then, adding soothing harmonies. I reached my hands and arms out to my sides, feeling the cool grass on my skin.

Turning my head to the side, I saw Darius sitting with his legs crossed in front of him, calmly looking out over the edge of the hill's drop off where green rolling hills stretched as far as the eye could see. Behind him, Anders lay partially reclined, reading a book, his mop of black hair falling in front of his eyes. And a few feet to his side sat James, fidgeting absentmindedly with his fingers. I closed my eyes; James's discomfort was palpable and I wanted to enjoy the peace and coolness of this day, especially as I did not anticipate there being many more like it.

Celia and Raela finished their song, but the quiet was quickly replaced by a friendly call from behind us. Propping myself up and turning in the direction of the village and village road, I saw our good friend, Agatha, and her fiancé, Gregory, making their way toward us.

"Sorry we missed the picnic earlier. Gregory and I had some wedding plans to discuss with Mr. Thomas," Agatha said as she approached, her shoulder-length, mousy brown hair blowing around her face.

"Well, we're glad you're here now," Celia said.

"So what kind of wedding plans did you discuss today?" I asked, pushing myself into a seated position as I noticed Anders close his book to join in the conversation.

"Food," Agatha replied. "As a new student of Harpson's Culinary Institute, I received a fairly generous banquet offer at a fantastic price," she stated proudly.

"Well that's good because I wasn't going to come unless the food was promised to be good," Darius joked, a small, playful smirk touching his broad face.

"Well, it's going to be!" Gregory happily chimed in. "We will be serving Carnelian crab, which happens to be my personal favorite."

"I love Carnelian crab," Celia, Raela, and I all said nearly simultaneously.

"Well what about the cake?" Anders asked. "That's your specialty after all."

"I know the exact types of chocolate I would like to be used, though I still have to find someone to make it. Unless I just decide to make it myself after all," Agatha said.

"Sarah, is that your father?" James cut in.

I turned around, and sure enough, climbing the hill from the village road was my father. His dark gray hair sporting a particularly disheveled look that day, his new half-moon glasses perched high up on his nose.

"Hello, Father. Do you need me at home?" I asked cheerily as he approached.

"Not just yet. I actually came for Anders. His family is looking for him," my father responded. His speech came out in his usually energetic tone, though his eyes looked tired and creased. Something was wrong, though I dared not ask about it in front of our entire group of friends.

Anders had stood up at once, not bothering to brush the dirt from his black pants. "See you later," he called, immediately following my father back down the hill.

"So anyway, I was thinking of using northern chocolate as the base for the cake," Agatha continued as they left. My thoughts remained with Anders, though. I hoped that his family members were all right, though I couldn't imagine what the problem would be. Like me, they couldn't really injure themselves or grow ill. They could, however, be discovered, and I worried that this was the case.

An hour later, the sun was beginning its slow descent toward the horizon. "I should go home now to make dinner," I said, standing and casually checking my gauzy white dress for grass stains.

"I should be going too," James added, jumping up. "I'll go back with you."

"All right," I casually accepted. "See you tomorrow?" I said to Celia, Raela, Darius, Agatha, and Gregory.

"See you tomorrow," Darius replied as the others nodded their heads or made throaty noises in affirmation.

As James and I walked down the hill, I could hear his heavy breathing. "Pull yourself together," I said quietly, out of earshot of the others.

"It's just, I feel like we betrayed the group," James replied. I turned my head toward him as we continued walking. Only a few inches taller than me, his straight brown eyebrows were drawn together as if in pain, and his normally pink skin looked a bit pale.

"We didn't betray anyone," I stated firmly.

"But we promised a long time ago that we wouldn't become involved with anyone in the group. We're all such good friends. What if our kiss destroys the group?"

I sighed. Poor James was always a worrier, but he seemed particularly distressed by what he perceived as our betrayal of our tight-knit group of friends.

"If they all find out, it will be awkward for everyone," he continued.

"Well, what does our kiss mean to you?" I asked, almost afraid of the answer.

"I—I don't know," he said, his blue eyes flashing alarm.

I was rather relieved that he didn't profess his undying love for me in response to my question. "Well, then just don't tell anyone. We can figure it out later if we want to."

In truth, I wasn't exactly sure why James and I had kissed the night before. It wasn't that I didn't care for him. I really did. But I had thought I cared for him like I cared for all of our friends. Then, the night before, we had all met at the lake a few minutes from my house. The night air was fresh, and we had all been seated beneath the willow tree, its leaves swaying ever so gently like feathers. The lights from the twinkling stars were reflected in the clear lake water, and everything just felt so peaceful. When our friends each started to excuse themselves one by one, I had found myself with no desire to leave. And so James and I had eventually found ourselves alone at the lake. Our conversation had quickly turned to what a glorious summer it had been, though we were sad that it would be over in just a few short weeks. It would be at that time that our close group would start to become separated from each other as each of us had different life paths we were choosing to take. Our feelings of nostalgia were strong as a result, I suppose, and before I realized what we were doing, our lips were touching. We didn't pull apart for at least a minute, with me wondering all the while what on earth I was doing. It had been a nice kiss, though I couldn't say I was ready to accept a marriage proposal by him, and so I had planned on acting as if it had not happened, hoping he would do the same. I should have known James would never be able to keep calm with such a secret weighing him down.

"I just feel like now that the two of us have kissed, we aren't the same group of friends we once were," James reiterated.

We were nearly to the front of my house, and I stopped and turned my whole body toward him. "You're right, James. We aren't the same group of friends we once were. And that has nothing to do with us kissing last night." His eyebrows rose in surprise and question, his thin lips clamped shut. "We've all grown up, we've all changed. And things are about to change a lot more. Agatha is getting married. And as a result Gregory is now part of our group when he wasn't before. And you don't think other spouses will join us eventually? We didn't destroy the group, and the group is going to continue to change whether the two of us never speak to each other again or get married."

James nodded his head seriously. "You're right. I'm overreacting. Just with everyone about to start different career paths and lives, I'm just a bit nervous I suppose."

I suddenly regretted being perhaps too blunt with him, and I gently placed my hand on his shoulder and gave him what I hoped was a comforting smile. "It's all right, James. Just don't worry about it for now, and let's enjoy the rest of our summer together."

"All right," he agreed, the trace of a smile lighting his face. "See you tomorrow?" he asked.

"See you tomorrow," I responded, and I turned and opened the short fence in front of my house as he continued to walk past it in the direction of his own home.

"Just—," he called back before I reached my front door, "can we not tell anyone about it?"

"Sure, James," I said, and I placed my hand on the door handle and went inside.

"Father!" I called.

"I'll be with you in a bit, Sarah," he responded from the back of the house where his study was located. Walking toward the open door, I saw that Anders was in the room with him, along with his mother, father, and younger sister. Their backs were to me, but their postures were quite rigid. Not wanting to intrude, I walked out the back door. The sun was quite low now, and the yard was cast in long shadows. I walked past the chicken pen to our tiny barn where we kept our donkey. Stepping inside, I threw some fresh hay into his stall. Crunching around in the loose hay strewn about the floor, I reached for some treats for him when the open barn door was darkened by a figure. I turned and saw Anders standing there, his unusually tall, though somewhat lanky form blocking out a lot of the remaining light.

"So," he said, leaning against the door frame and allowing some of the sunlight back inside, "are you pregnant or something?"

Chapter Two

My mouth dropped open and then I immediately looked downward, wondering if my dress looked too puffy; like my mother had, I despised corsets, but was naturally thin enough to not attract attention to this disdain.

Anders laughed at this. "No, you don't look fat."

"Well then, what is your pregnancy comment in reference to?" I demanded, just a bit angered.

"James," he responded, and I felt my mouth drop open again. "I haven't heard the poor kid that worried since he accidentally ran over Mrs. Tine's chicken with that cart."

"So you do listen to our fears?" I said, not entirely shocked, but more surprised that he was acknowledging it.

"It's sometimes hard not to," he said casually, though he eyed me carefully, seemingly scrutinizing my face for a reaction. "Plus, James is so constant in his worrying, and he was sitting right next to me. I tried to read a book to tune him out, but that was no help. So, that brings me back to my previous question. Are you pregnant or something, because based on James's worries, I'm guessing you two have triplets on the way."

I frowned at Anders and shot him what I hoped was a look of warning. "Careful there," I said. "No. I'm not pregnant."

"Well then, what on earth is he so worried about?" Anders asked, and as I stepped closer to him, his brown eyes brightly reflected a bit of the vanishing sunlight.

"We kissed last night. Nothing more. And quite honestly, I don't think it meant anything to either of us."

"Well why did you kiss him then?" he asked genuinely.

"I don't know," I said, almost coming out as a whine. "Right place, wrong person?"

"Ah," Anders said. "Well, the poor guy was worried to death that we would all find out about it somehow. Especially Raela for whatever reason, but that is neither here nor there. I wanted to find you and talk to you about what your father just told me and my family."

As curious as I was about Anders' purposeful tidbit about Raela, I was much more anxious as to why my father had had the entire Stone family in his study.

Anders stepped inside the tiny barn then and sat down on a stool. I first lit a candle against the growing darkness and then sat down on a stool next to him. Anders looked more serious than usual. He wasn't one for big smiles, his pale skin and black hair always lending him a very slight melancholy look. Still, his eyes always shined with playfulness, and you could just tell by watching him that he was happily listening to every single word, and maybe even thought, around him.

I was only partially comfortable around Anders, even though we had been friends for years. His family had bought the house next to mine about four years prior, when we were fourteen years old. He had been very shy at first, staying largely by himself at school. Meanwhile, I was already close to my same group of friends. About a month after his family's arrival, I remember us all watching him eat by himself in the village square.

"So tell us about your new neighbor," I could remember Agatha asking me eagerly as our group ate together, our usual animated raucousness present.

"He hasn't really said much to me," I responded. This was true, but I had already known more about him than I was willing to share with my friends.

Two weeks prior to that, I had come home one afternoon to find his family in our sitting room with my father. "Sarah," my father had greeted me happily. "Have you met any of the Stone family yet?"

"I've seen them around, but haven't had the pleasure of meeting any of them yet. Hello," I said, staring at each of their faces in turn. Mr. Stone was tall and thin, his black hair and dark brown eyes popping against his pale skin. His mother's skin was a bit tanner in complexion, though she too was tall with black hair. Anders' sister, Molly, was seven at the time, and she was the only member of the family showing off brown hair, though like her father and brother, she too was particularly pale. And then there was fourteen-year-old Anders, shyly avoiding eye contact with me, much the same in appearance to his older self, though considerably shorter.

I took a seat in a wooden chair next to my father, the entire Stone family seated opposite him on our exceptionally long, lumpy sofa.

"Sarah, you know how you don't tell anyone that you are a Hersote?" my father then asked seemingly out of nowhere. I looked in panic at the Stones, though I knew that there was a reason my father was bringing this up in front of them. "Well, the Stones here have a similar secret that they need us to keep."

"I do hope you don't mind, but I thought that since we have some things in common, it might be nice to share the burden of our secrets with each other," Mrs. Stone said, her voice melodic and comforting. I relaxed slightly and maintained eye contact with her as she continued. "We are Slytons." My body grew rigid again for a brief moment.

Slytons, like Hersotes, were immortal. Only there were some very important differences between these only two known immortal groups of people. Hersotes were usually magic users, and it was through a perfection of their magic that they had achieved immortality on our earth. My mother had been one, and had passed this trait on to me through birth. My father was a Lellio, a mortal magic user. There were other types of people in our world, most of them non-magical: The Shermonos from the north of our huge country of Lystia, the woodsy Jersos from the far east, and our friends, the Losos from the south and west hill and sea regions. The Slytons, though, were rare and belonged to no specific region or country in our world. Arguably, they didn't belong in our world at all. Many said that they belonged only in hell, though these were often the same people who would argue that this was the proper place for the unnatural Hersotes as well. Still, the Slytons did harbor what might be classified as evil powers. They had the ability to clearly hear and perceive any of the fears going through the minds of the people around them. In this way, they could make a formidable foe. Dark secrets weren't safe around them.

Adding to their sinister reputation, they had the chilling ability to enter doors to hell on the nights of full moons. These invisible doors apparently appeared throughout the earth, offering a way both in to hell and out for those Slytons already living in that horrible underworld. Still, not all Slytons embraced this ability to travel between worlds, and at that time I was sincerely hoping that my new neighbors were among those that despised their heritage to hell.

"Don't worry," Mrs. Stone said immediately. "We don't align ourselves with those Slytons that acknowledge hell as their home," she added, probably reading my fears. But there was still the fact that they would be able to hear all of my other fears. *You'll still be able to hear about how I killed my mother. Accidentally, but nevertheless, I killed her,* I couldn't help but think.

Mrs. Stone's expression was the only one whose didn't change at this thought. Mr. Stone's eyebrows raised in surprise, but only for a split second. Molly looked frightened, though her childlike features were easy to ignore. Anders' reaction, on the other hand, was the most noteworthy to me. He looked up at me cautiously, making direct eye contact. The eyes I found so playful later on looked at me pitifully. He then threw me a small smile before withdrawing his eye contact again. It was not a smile of enjoyment, but one of comfort, turned up just slightly at one corner of his mouth. Meanwhile, his mother only hesitated a moment before continuing, "Don't worry. All of your deepest fears are safe with us," she said, giving my father a comforting smile then.

"They actually came to ask for my help, Sarah," my father continued as if nothing tense had occurred at all. "You've probably heard, on the nights of full moons, Slytons can see the doors to hell that are invisible to us. The Stones have no desire to enter these doors, though the urge to do so on the nights of full moons is strong."

"The full moons bring out the worst possible versions of ourselves," Mrs. Stone gently cut in.

"So," my father continued, "I'm going to help them each night of the full moon by locking them in their house and freeing them the next morning when the danger for them has passed."

"I see," I responded.

"Perhaps we can all become good friends. After all," Mrs. Stone said, looking at me, "like us, you'll be around for a very, very long time." She smiled at me, and I felt relaxed in her motherly gaze.

Still, there was something much more intimidating about befriending a Slyton my own age, and so even though their family stayed and talked pleasantly with us all that evening, I never made an attempt to talk one-on-one with Anders. So when Agatha spotted Anders in the square a couple of weeks later, I wasn't eager to bring him over.

"Oh, come on. He's so mysterious looking, and easy on the eyes," she said.

"Yea, what are you waiting for?" Celia had asked.

"I could always use another guy to talk to. James doesn't count," Darius teased.

"What's that supposed to mean?" James said, growing red in the face. He never was good at receiving playful jabs.

"Teasing. Just teasing," Darius said.

I could hardly tell my friends that Anders was a Slyton and that he would be able to hear all of our fears. It was too big a secret to spill to anyone, even my closest friends. And so I crossed the village square and stood next to where Anders was seated on a bench, staring intently at his lunch. He didn't look up at me until I was right next to him.

"Hi, Anders. Would you like to come sit with me and my friends?" I asked hesitantly.

He had given me a little smile and responded, "That's all right. I don't want to make you uncomfortable." He then looked back down at his lunch and took another bite.

I took a deep breath. "Seriously, Anders. It's all right."

He looked up at me, taking his time in swallowing the food in his mouth as he stared at me thoughtfully. He then silently stood, my eyes slightly above his at that age. "Just so you know, I won't reference anyone's fears, and I'll just try my best to ignore what I hear in the first place." I nodded and smiled, and the two of us walked over to my boisterously waiting friends. And ever since that day, he had been a part of our group.

Nevertheless, Anders and I almost never found ourselves alone. Truthfully, this was largely by my design, especially as my past fears and regrets were not of the simple nature of the accidental chicken murder that apparently bothered James so deeply. So this time in the barn with just Anders was odd to begin with, much less the fact that he had so plainly acknowledged James's fear from that day. Still, as he sat with such a serious expression on his face, I had a feeling that that was only the surface of unusual for the day.

"Your father told my family of a special full moon that is expected, about three months from now," he began. "It's called a blood moon." He was quiet then, looking at me seriously, letting the words sink in.

I froze, the memories that haunted me of my mother's death coming back to me full force.

"I'm guessing your father is going to tell you about the moon too, but I thought I should let you know about it, just in case he doesn't plan to tell you. Your father—he doesn't ever worry about the moon or fear what you did. You know, what happened to you I mean, that night. Not that I know all of the details, just what you've feared about being responsible for your mother's death." He looked a bit uncomfortable himself, though he was obviously being as delicate as possible while not hiding the facts.

"What did my father tell you about the blood moon?" I asked, my throat suddenly dry.

"He warned us about it, since my family doesn't have a good reaction to full moons to begin with. This full blood moon, though…my family is not sure how it will affect us. According to your father, there hasn't been one in more than two thousand years. My mother wasn't even alive yet. But our parents seemed to think that this blood moon will make us angrier and more desperate than ever to enter one of the doors to hell. I suppose they'll look into what precautions we should take in the meantime. But…I wanted to let you know because I didn't know what precautions you might need to take too."

I nodded thoughtfully, no longer looking at Anders but focusing on the plain wooden wall in front of us. "Yes. Thank you. I—I honestly don't know what to do."

"Well, you have several months to think about it," Anders said, rising from his stool. He turned and looked back at me from the doorway. "Good night, Sarah."

"Good night, Anders," I said, and I watched his tall figure walk off in the direction of his house.

I didn't know what I should do to prepare myself, if I would kill accidentally again at another blood moon. And Anders had said my father had said a blood moon hadn't occurred for more than two thousand years. Had my father not looked at the sky when my mother had died? I decided to sleep on my thoughts and fears, and so after only a few minutes in the barn by myself, I rose, blew out the candle, and went inside my house.

I found my father shucking corn inside. "Hello, Sarah," he said cheerily. "How was your picnic today?"

"Fine," I said distractedly.

My father stopped and looked at me. "I saw Anders go toward the barn. Did he tell you about the blood moon?" My father had never once referenced the blood moon to me. He only told me that my mother's death had been a confusing phenomenon that he had previously thought impossible. But he had promised me that he would protect me with his life, as if I were afraid of killing myself. He had it backwards, I had been afraid of accidentally killing him, and that was still my fear this night.

"Don't worry about the Stones," my father continued after I simply nodded in answer to his question. "We'll all work together to figure out what precautions they should take. In the meantime, why don't you tell me more about your picnic?" he said, and he continued shucking corn.

Though he had at least directly mentioned the blood moon to me, it was clear that he had no further intentions of discussing its impact with me.

Chapter Three

We had walked more than an hour north, where the hills instead grew mountainous and the lakes and streams more plentiful. "This had better be worth the hike," Agatha lightly complained, huffing and puffing as we climbed higher up a steep path, her tiny shoulders heaving as she breathed.

"I've been here once before. It was beautiful," Darius promised, his massive body perspiring noticeably, but his breathing as calm and even as always.

Shortly afterward, we could hear the sounds of rushing water grow louder, and another minute later the trees opened up into a beautiful oasis. There was a pond before us, which was fed by a thin but beautiful waterfall, perhaps one hundred feet in height. The pond, in turn, fed a small river. The day was cloudless and clear.

"This is beautiful, Darius," I said, stepping to the water's edge where a light mist sprayed me from the waterfall.

"It really is," Anders agreed, coming up alongside me with Raela.

When I turned around, Celia was already laying out a blanket and Agatha was unpacking one of three large picnic baskets we had brought with us.

We all began helping and in no time we were seated in this beautiful paradise, ready to enjoy this last big day we had planned together.

"I know there is still a week left until the first of us has to leave," Darius spoke, eyeing Celia and Raela, "but I thought we should take this opportunity to toast each of us. This last week is going to be a busy one, and we might not all be together again until Agatha and Gregory's wedding. And so, may I start a series of toasts?" he said, raising his metal mug and all of us following his lead.

He turned toward the first person on his left. "To James. He may not be going far away, but becoming the new village school master is a worthy and noble task, and one that I'm sure he is ready for. The best of us in school, I'm sure he will find the work fulfilling and change the lives of many future pupils. To James!"

"To James!" we all repeated, and took a sip of our honey juice.

"You next James?" Darius asked, nodding toward the person on his left.

"Oh? Sure," James said, turning to face Raela. "Raela, we couldn't be more proud of you. We always love listening to your enchanting voice. Your harmonies with your sister are truly beautiful. And although we are going to miss hearing you sing at every village festival, the court at Harpson is lucky to have such an addition to their royal singers. We will miss you. Very much. To Raela!"

"To Raela!" we all repeated.

Raela then turned toward her own sister. "Well Celia," she said, tucking a strand of her smooth brown hair behind her ear as she looked at her nearly identical sister. "You have the sweetest melodies of any singer I know. I'm blessed to call you my sister, and excited that we both get to go to Harpson together in a week. I never doubted for a moment that you would be chosen to be one of the royal singers. To our next great adventure together. To Celia!"

"To Celia!"

"Well, I guess I get to talk about dear Agatha now," Celia said, smiling at our friend. "Agatha, I'm so glad you'll be going to the capital with us. Not because I care about you, but because your baking is to die for." We all laughed and Agatha blushed. "In all seriousness, I'm glad that we'll be in the same city as you and your sweet smile and kind heart. I know you'll find success at the Culinary Institute, and you have to remember to send all of us cookies on a regular basis. To Agatha!"

"To Agatha!"

"Well I guess I'm the lucky one who gets to toast my fiancé," Agatha said, smiling at him with her mouth and her eyes. "Gregory, I'm so glad that you asked me to our village dance last year. I couldn't imagine my life without you. I'm excited for the journey we are going to make together to Harpson soon where you'll start your life as the best general goods shop owner in the country. I love you. To Gregory!"

"To Gregory!"

"My turn then to toast Sarah," Gregory said. "Sarah, you have a direct, but fun and kind of bouncy way about life, and I'm sure we'll find those same qualities in your clothing. Mrs. Strawn is the best seamstress in the village, and after apprenticing under her, I'm sure you'll come to steal that title in no time. By the way, did you sew this?" Gregory asked, only half joking as he pointed to my lavender sundress.

"Of course," I answered, smiling at our friend's fiancé.

"Well, if this is the kind of clothing you create, you're going to truly make a name for yourself. To Sarah!"

"To Sarah!"

I turned to my left then. It was Anders' turn. "Well, Anders," I said, only to pause for a few seconds. In truth, I knew more about him than all of my friends, and yet I couldn't say even half of what I wanted to in a toast.

Darius coughed loudly. "There's got to be something nice you can come up with," he said loudly in the middle of yet another fake cough, and everyone laughed.

"It's not that," I defended myself while laughing. "I just didn't know where to start."

Anders smirked at me, his face full of pleasant mischief.

"Anders," I began again. "We're all really going to miss you. You're the thinker of this group and you pay attention to every little detail. You're going to make a fine soldier. I'm sure you'll find success in the military."

I knew his family was actually quite unhappy with his decision to join the military, as they feared his Slyton identity would be discovered quite quickly. He had argued that if anyone should join the Lystian army, it should be an immortal. Plus, he said he would have plenty of time to change his career. After all, he had all of the time in the world.

"To summarize, Anders, be safe, and we'll miss you. Unless you're stationed near our village, of course, which I'm definitely hoping for even though there aren't any active bases near us and we aren't in a war."

"Way to be wordy," Darius joked under his breath.

I pursed my lips in mock anger. "To Anders!" I finished.

"To Anders!"

Anders turned toward Darius. "Darius, you've already made a name for yourself as a blacksmith. You started your apprenticeship young, and it paid off. Now, you already have orders from the Harpson military even though you plan to remain in the village, and I hope to be issued one of your fine weapons myself. Your talent will surely make you a great name. Congratulations on your success already and may it continue. To Darius!"

"To Darius!" we all echoed, and we drained our honey juice.

After our picnic lunch, we all decided to climb to the top of the waterfall. The way was extremely rocky and slippery, and I kept glancing back to be sure tiny Agatha was all right, though it seemed that Gregory was helping her climb carefully and safely to the top.

It took fifteen minutes of carefully navigating the seldom-used path to the top portion of the waterfall cliff, but the view was beautiful.

"Good suggestion, Darius," Anders said. "A perfect spot to have our last get together."

"Don't say that!" Celia said. "It sounds so sad to say it's our last one."

"Our last for the time being, "Anders amended.

The waterfall crashed to our right, creating tiny rainbows in its mist below.

"We can move a bit closer right?" Raela asked.

"A bit," Darius agreed. "Though just be careful because the path is very narrow between the mountain edge and the drop off."

"We'll wait here," Gregory piped up, staring at his obviously nervous bride-to-be.

"All right. We'll be right back," James said, and the rest of us continued on.

We only walked a minute when the path became too pebbly and narrow to continue safely, and the waterfall fell only ten feet or so to our side in any case.

"It really is beautiful," I said as we all stared down and out at the rushing water.

"Well, let's head back to Agatha and Gregory," Darius said after a minute.

I took only one step in that direction when I felt odd, almost dizzy. It took another second for me to realize that it was not my own body's uncertainty, but the ground beneath me, shifting. It was another second after that before Anders cried, "Earthquake!" and the ground began to groan wildly.

We had only ever experienced one other earthquake in our lifetime, and we had all been very young. I barely remembered it, though I did remember that no serious damage was done as our buildings in the village were all fairly short, and the rolling hills could hardly topple onto us.

Here, though, the earth grumbled beneath us, and it was easy to lose our footing on the loose pebbles. Just as I realized that Anders had dropped to the ground in front of me to avoid toppling over the edge, I lost my own footing and fell to the right, directly over the path and into the array of vines and uneven rocks making up the slippery drop-off next to the waterfall. Although I had firm hold of one of the vines and was only a foot down from the edge of the path, the earth continued to sway and I really thought that I was going to plunge right down to the bottom where the earth churned from the waterfall and the rocks pointed jaggedly upward at us.

It couldn't have lasted more than a minute, but I felt weak and shaky by the time the quaking slowed, and I felt disoriented by the screams of my friends. Finally feeling the earth come to a general stop, I looked to my right and then my left. I almost screamed in response to what I saw there—Celia dangling from a vine like mine perhaps six feet to my right and a few feet lower. "Hold on, Celia!" I said, eyeing the vines around me and the rocks where I could place my feet.

She didn't turn her head toward me, didn't move at all except to quake in place as if the earthquake were still moving her.

"Sarah! Give me your hand!" I looked up and saw James there, prostrate on the ground, his hand held out for mine.

"I'm fine! Get Celia!" I responded.

"Just give me your hand first!"

"No! Get Celia now."

And James, clearly confused, but needing to act quickly, slid his body to the side where Raela and Darius were trying to pull vines out of the rock to lower to Celia.

Meanwhile, Anders dropped over the side, almost carelessly, holding onto rocks and vines between Celia and me. "Here I come Celia!" he said. "Just hold on."

"Careful Anders," Darius said, shock evident in his voice.

"I'm fine. Just hold on, Celia," Anders continued, his voice calm, but his actions deliberate and quick.

He managed to navigate a foot downward. "Grab hold of my pant leg," he said. I saw her reach for it feebly, but then cling back to the vine.

"I can't," she said, her voice barely audible above the crashing waterfall.

My heart stuttered then as I felt the earth vibrate again. I had been looking in the direction of Celia, though she was blocked from my view by Anders. Still, the small aftershock must have been too much. Anders cried, "Celia!" and lunged for her. I tried to do my part and lunged for Anders to help hold them both up, but I was too weak and too slow. We were falling, all three of us, toward the rocks below. I barely processed the screams from our friends above before we hit the ground.

It felt strange, but not painful. Almost tingly. For the briefest of moments I couldn't breathe or move, or even think. But then all at once, I was fine. I sat myself up and looked to my left where Anders was also sitting up, his back unflexing from the pointy rock on which he had landed. He spared the briefest of glances for me before turning to his left. "Sarah, don't look," he said loudly and seriously. He then rushed over the side of the rock to the shallow water. I obeyed his directive; I didn't want to have the memory of Celia's body after that fall.

Chapter Four

I covered my face with a delicate black veil. I hoped that no one at the funeral would be able to recognize me, but logic knew not to hope for such a thing.

I tied a black ribbon around the center of my waist and looked in the mirror. I was torn between going and not going to the funeral. I didn't want to go and see my friends and Celia's family. Not after what had happened. But not going to Celia's funeral felt wrong. I took a deep breath and stepped out of my bedroom.

Down the hall, my father was still in his study, the door open invitingly.

Hearing my footsteps, he turned around at his desk. "You're sure you want to go?" he asked delicately.

"I have to. She was my friend," I said, to which my father nodded in understanding.

"And you're sure you don't want me to go?" he asked.

"It's going to be hard enough to avoid becoming a spectacle with just me and Anders going. No need to draw you into it too."

My father nodded again. "I love you. I'll see you soon," he said, and he turned his gray head back to his books at his desk.

I stood and watched him for a few seconds before departing. At eighteen, I was taller than my father now. I had been ever since sixteen perhaps. And while his face was wrinkle-free, his gray hair spoke of his aging.

While Lellios were not generally feared or despised by the other mortals, they were often considered powerful due to their ability to wield magic. Still, the magic was often not particularly powerful, and usually limited to one type depending on the person. My father's particular brand of magic was focused on light. He could ignite candles and even entice a star or two to twinkle just a bit brighter for a moment. He was fascinated by the celestial bodies, which explained his interest in the upcoming blood moon.

And despite his knowledge and small powers, he appeared to me in that moment weak and fragile. He would die one day. He would have died had he been the one to fall from that cliff. He would continue to grow older, and one day he would have wrinkles, and maybe even white hair. His back would start to ache and he would have to say goodbye to me.

As I had taken after my immortal Hersote mother, I also presumably had the ability to wield magic. My father had offered to teach me when I reached the age of ten, but I had refused to learn more deeply about any kind of magic, let alone discover my own type. After all, I had presumably wielded magic once before, and it had resulted in the death of my immortal mother. I wanted nothing to do with magic. And so the only thing I had allowed my father to explain to me was that once I reached an age that I was happy with, I could simply decide to stay there. My mother had chosen to stay at twenty-three, so she would always keep the body, wrinkle-free face, and straight posture of that age.

I hadn't chosen to stop my aging yet. There was supposed to come a time, I knew, when I should have to say goodbye to my friends and disappear lest they discover my Hersote heritage. I had liked to think that my friends would be different, that they would embrace Anders' and my immortality. Recent events had proven otherwise.

I walked out of my front door and found Anders waiting for me, uncomfortably kicking at the dirt at my front gate.

"You could have come inside," I said as I reached him.

"I figured you'd be along in a minute," he said quietly, and the two of us walked down the road together, headed for the far hill on this side of town that held the village cemetery.

We walked in silence. For a brief, absurd moment, I wanted nothing more than to reach out and take Anders' hand for comfort, but I kept walking, our heads bent, looking at the road in front of us.

We had walked in this subdued way for much of the return trip from the waterfall. As soon as they had descended from the waterfall path, Darius picked up the picnic blanket, which he used to wrap Celia's body. He then immediately turned for home, the others right behind him, sparing only disgusted looks in our direction.

We had waited perhaps an hour in silence then, sitting on the rocks.

"We tried," I had finally spoken.

"I know."

"And now we've lost all of our friends."

"I know," he said again, swallowing hard. "Let's go home," he finally said, and taking my hand at that time, we had walked home in silence.

We had stayed in our houses all the next day, though my father spent a large portion of it out of the house, presumably fielding questions by the villagers who were nervous about Anders' and my newly discovered identities.

Far ahead of us, we saw the cemetery hill come into view, and the thick group of mourners located there. Having planned to arrive late, we hoped to blend in with the back of the group and then leave undetected. As we started to climb the hill, Anders quietly whispered to me, "Are you leaving the village?"

"Father and I have barely talked about it. Why? Are you?" I asked, suddenly panicked at the thought of not having the Stones near me.

"Probably, but we haven't firmed up any details just yet," he whispered back, but then we had to be quiet, as we were growing close to the group.

Stepping up to the back as planned, we could hear the minister speaking in drawn-out, sorrowful speech. "And so Lord, we thank you for the blessing of our dear Celia, and thank You that she is in a better place now."

We couldn't see the minister from our position, but there was a shift in the group of people, working its way back from those in the front, and we assumed it was time for everyone to file past the coffin, laid in the ground, but not yet covered over with earth. And so we jostled a bit with those around us, keeping my veiled face low while Anders pulled his black hat down a little further in front of his eyes. We continued to shuffle around as a makeshift line was formed.

As we grew closer to the coffin I could feel people's eyes on us. Anders whispered the answer to my fears, "Yes. Some people are starting to notice us."

I silently nodded my head and kept walking toward the coffin.

Upon reaching it, a voice finally rang out loudly. "What are you doing here?" It was a melodic voice, even in its apparent anger, and I looked up to see Raela and Celia's younger sister standing near the coffin with her family, her eyes focused on Anders and me, creased in anger.

"We've just come to pay respect to our friend," Anders stated firmly, but softly.

I was looking at the family out of the corner of my eye. Her mother was crying silent tears and was unusually pale while her father was glaring in our direction with bright red cheeks. The sister—I thought I remembered her being fifteen now—was still staring at us with anger, her fists clenched tightly at her sides. And then there was Raela, avoiding our gaze altogether, focused instead on the coffin in the earth.

"You're not welcome here," the sister said again. "Leave here with my sister's life force, you unthankful scum."

We had not desired to make a scene at Celia's funeral, and so, passing as respectfully as possible by the coffin, we continued back down the hill and away from the ongoing service.

Celia and Raela's sister had expressed one of the more common misconceptions about immortals—that we supposedly fed on the life force of mortals through their deaths. The assumption, therefore, would be that on some level we were pleased that Celia had died so that we might keep living forever. This could not have been further from the truth.

"I hate that thought," Anders said as we reached the village path below once more.

"What?" I asked, surprised to hear a normal vocal volume once more.

"That we like the deaths of mortals. That stupid life force trash," he continued, and upon glancing at him, I saw that the color was high in his usually pale face. Like the singers' sister, his fists were also clenched at his sides.

Stopping, I reached out at once for his fists. He let his hands unfurl in mine. "Anders, we know that's not true. We tried our best to save Celia. We both cared for her, and whatever horrible things they choose to believe doesn't change that."

Anders' head was pointed down, focused on his hands in mine. His eyes were watery, but not shedding tears. He heaved a deep, almost painful sigh and continued walking, keeping his one hand firmly in mine.

Reaching my front gate, he gave my hand a final squeeze, and we silently parted ways.

Opening my front door, the smell of gingerbread found its way to my nostrils, a homey, pleasant spell standing in sharp contrast to the day I was having.

My father stepped out of the kitchen into the front room. "Back so soon?" he asked, his gray eyebrows scrunched low over his spectacles.

"Yes," I said quietly. "We paid our respects, though as expected, we weren't welcome."

My father bit his lip anxiously before responding, overly happy in tone, "I'm making you gingerbread! Something to cheer you up a bit!"

"Thanks," I said, and I wandered hazily toward the kitchen where the scent wafted from our ancient metal oven.

While I stared at the heavy, opaque door, my father walked up behind me, laying his hand gently on my shoulder. "I know this is awful now, but things will be all right."

In opposition to his comforting words, my whole body let out a shudder. "This is all just so awful. I loved Celia like a sister," I croaked, beginning to lose control on the tears I had held at bay all day. "And now none of my friends are talking to me, except for Anders, of course."

"I know," my father said sadly. "People just fear what is different from them."

"Well, perhaps people should fear me," I said, a hint of resentful anger creeping in. "Especially with this stupid blood moon coming."

"I already told you, sweetheart, that I'll do my best to protect all of the Stones during the blood moon."

"What about you?" I said, turning toward my father, the tears finally falling from my eyes in a steady stream. "What if I kill you, or even the Stones for that matter?"

My father's eyes popped open wide over his half-moon spectacles. "What? Kill me? What are you talking about?"

"Accidentally, of course," I said, a bit taken aback by his reaction. "With the blood moon, I mean."

"What are you talking about?"

"Like how I killed Mother," I said, blubbering heavily over my words.

I dropped my gaze to the floor, staring at my black leather shoes. When I looked back up at my father a minute later, I found a face stretched into shock, void of color. I was no Slyton, but I thought I could feel the fear emanating from his body.

"Sarah," he began slowly, "you think you killed your mother?"

I felt the blood drain from my own face then as my tears immediately came to a halt. "With the blood moon. How I accidentally sent the magic to kill her." I said, my voice emitting the words with a raspy, strangled sound.

"Sarah, I don't know what you saw or think you did back on that island, but there was no blood moon. It was daylight, sweetheart." He was eyeing me warily. "Perhaps you are having memories of a bad dream that you've come to think of as a memory of real life."

I stared at him, dumbfounded. "No, when we climbed that hill, I stepped on a stone and everything went dark and the moon came out and turned to blood." I was talking quickly now, and my words continued to pick up speed. "And then Mother called out to me and as I called back the blood fell from the moon and shot toward Mother, and when I saw her the front of her dress still had some of the blood on it, and she was dead."

My father started coughing then, violently, bending over as he did so. For a moment I thought he was going to be sick. Then he finally forced out, "Sarah, it was always daylight to me, and your mother simply collapsed on the path and died."

Black spots started swirling in front of my eyes, and I thought I was going to pass out. "I need to go lie down," I muttered, and I stumbled to my bedroom and locked the door. My father didn't try to come after me.

I lay down on my bed. It was stuffy in my room, but I didn't move to open the window that looked out on the backyard.

My father was never afraid of whatever powers I had used because he simply hadn't known I had wielded them, I realized. I suddenly looked at my whole childhood differently: my father's confusion when I didn't want to learn magic, him misunderstanding my fear of the moon for disinterest in his hobby.

I didn't move from my bed even after the sun began to set. As darkness began to creep up, I rose only to light a candle and relieve myself in the pan beneath my bed, not desiring to leave my room and face my father. Lying back down on my bed, I idly watched the shadows dance on my ceiling from the candle. I didn't know what to do; I couldn't bear the thought of facing my father, my old friends, or the people from the village again. I wanted today to be over, and yet tomorrow seemed to offer no more hope for a better day.

The single candlestick I had lit finally started to grow low as there was a quiet knock on my door. "Sarah," my father called gently. "I'm here for you when you're ready to talk."

I didn't respond at first. I could see the shadow of his feet on the other side of my bedroom door. Only after they shifted hesitantly did I quietly say, "Thank you, but I'm not ready yet."

"All right," he quietly said, and I saw his feet move away and then I heard his own bedroom door close down the hall.

A few minutes later, the candle burned out, and I fell asleep.

It had been a deep, dreamless sleep, and I felt surprisingly refreshed when I awoke to a faint tapping noise. I was surprised then to find my room covered in darkness, as my body had had the feeling of being asleep longer than I must have been. I looked around my dark room, the moon's light being almost non-existent on what I assumed was a very cloudy night.

Hearing the tapping noise again, I pushed myself upright in my bed, only to jump with surprise by a face only a foot away from my own, on the other side of my bedroom window. Thankfully, I had the presence of mind not to yell in fright, and squinting at the person in the dark, I quickly made out the angled nose and straight jawline of Anders.

Making eye contact with him, he quickly motioned for me to open the window. I of course complied immediately. "What are you doing here?" I whispered to him, my voice sounding loud in the silence, nonetheless.

"I have an idea," he said, suddenly climbing through my bedroom window awkwardly, his long legs making him appear like a giant spider in the shadows.

I backed away to let him in, as unorthodox as this midnight meeting was.

"Here it is," he said, and his voice sounded almost excited in the quiet.

"Shh," I warned him. Although Anders' voice wasn't quite as deep as the hulking Darius, I was a bit concerned that his more masculine tones would alert my sleeping father. Although we weren't engaged in anything inappropriate, I still wasn't sure how I would explain Anders' unusual presence in my bedroom in the middle of the night.

"Here's what I need to know first," Anders began again, marginally quieter. He drew close to me then, "I know you saw a blood moon when your mother died, but I don't know the details of what happened or where it was. If you can...I need you to tell me about it. All of it."

"Why? And why right now?" I said, shocked and a bit sickened at his request.

"Please, Sarah," he said.

I inhaled slowly, and sat down on the side of the bed, where he sat next to me with an unexpected amount of ease and comfort. "I was six at the time," I began quietly.

Chapter Five

I told the tale in what probably amounted to half an hour in as much detail as I could remember. I saw Anders nod his head occasionally as I spoke, his face bathed in shadow, making it difficult to decipher his reactions to my words.

"So why did you need to know all of that?" I finally asked, breaking the brief silence that had followed my story.

"I obviously didn't know all of the details. I only knew that you feared you were responsible for your mother's death, that you were afraid you would accidentally kill again, and that moons, in particular the thought of a blood moon, caused you much anxiety. I wanted to know how, and even if for that matter, you had seen a blood moon before. There hasn't exactly been one here recently. I'm just thinking, what if we go back to that island together?"

I was horrified. "What? For what purpose?"

"My mother and father haven't found anything about Slytons and blood moons in any of our books, so they're not sure what to expect. Also, you're not sure how the blood moon will affect you, if it does at all. The two of us are clearly not in a good location here. Let's go the two of us to this island and see what we can find out with what seems to be a blood moon you can summon at will."

"But—I'm not sure what it is. And what if I kill you?" I responded.

"I'll stay far back," he responded, and I thought he was being reckless in his thoughts and assumptions.

"That's silly. I'm not even sure if you'll be able to see the blood moon or if it will even reappear again. I think you're looking at this as a harmless, practice blood moon, and that's most definitely not what it was."

"Come on. Let's at least check it out together. Do you really want to stay around here?" he asked.

"No, but I feel like you're using this blood moon as an excuse to leave when it might very well be dangerous."

"Listen, Sarah," he said, his words suddenly measured and more serious than excited. "It's true. I don't want to stay here, and I would love to feel like I'm doing something—anything—productive right now. But I truly am concerned about the blood moon. And if we find this place, we can make sure we take all of the necessary precautions—for you too; don't forget that I become the worst version of myself during a regular full moon. But I really would like to see if there are any answers at this place—for both of us."

I sighed. "I don't even know how to find it," I whispered. "It took us more than a week to get there and it was in the west. But I was six. I really don't remember anything more than that. And my father took the map and threw it into the sea on our way back home. And I can hardly imagine he'd want to help me find that horrible island again."

"Let's go to Ballos Port and start there. Maybe someone's heard of it," he said, beginning to grow uncharacteristically excited again.

I looked around my dark room. I could understand his desperateness to leave with the current atmosphere in our village. I sighed. "When did you want to leave?"

"Now."

"Now?"

"Yes. Why not?"

I sighed again, resigning myself to his enthusiasm. "Just give me a few minutes to change my clothing," I said, realizing that I had not even taken my black shoes off from the funeral earlier.

"All right," he said, and he jumped up and made his way over to my still-open window.

"Does your family know?" I asked just as he began to climb out.

"You've got to be kidding. Of course not," he said, and I couldn't see the expression on his face. "You're not telling your father, are you?"

"No way. He'd die of shock if he knew."

"All right. I'll be right outside your window when you're ready," he said, and he climbed out.

Trusting that Anders wouldn't peek into my room, I quickly undressed and put on a brown summer dress, gauzy but with many layers. I then put on my most comfortable pair of brown work shoes. I considered packing a bag, but having not seen one with Anders, decided that this would be a voyage with only the most basic of necessities—the clothes on our backs and a pocketful of cash from my dresser.

In a most unladylike way with my longer than average limbs, I climbed out of my window, shutting it quietly behind me. The moon and stars were completely concealed by the heavy clouds above, and I glanced around my dark yard for a moment looking for Anders. I was surprised then to hear his voice come from almost right next to me, in the deep shadows at the side of my house.

"Ready?" he whispered.

"Yes," I said, and I partially ran into him, realizing where he was standing a millisecond too late.

He took a few steps toward the side of my house, but then stopped in his tracks, with me plowing full force into his back this time.

"Why'd you stop?" I whispered, rubbing my nose as it had collided with the bones of his lower neck.

"Shh," he said quickly. "I hear someone."

I listened in the dark, but couldn't hear a thing. Even the wind was silent on this opaque summer night. "I don't hear anyone."

"He's not talking. He's just worried someone will see him," Anders replied. We were quiet for another few seconds. Finally, Anders said, "Darn it. I think it's James."

And then suddenly, Anders fell back into me as presumably James collided with him walking around the corner of my house.

"Who's there?" James whispered, panicked as we all stood back up.

"Anders and me," I answered.

"What are you doing out here?" James asked.

"I could ask you the same thing," I replied.

"I was coming to talk to you. I figured I'd check on you at your window."

"In eighteen years, no one has ever met me at my bedroom window, and now everyone wants to," I said, shaking my head in the dark.

"Huh?" James said.

"Never mind. What do you want, James?"

"Well, I'm glad you're both here actually. I just wanted to say that I'm not afraid of you both—with you being immortals, I mean. You tried to help Celia. It wasn't your fault, obviously."

There was silence for a few seconds. "Thank you, James," I finally said. "That means a lot."

"Why did you decide to come in the middle of the night?" Anders finally spoke.

"I...well, my parents aren't exactly of the same mind," he said awkwardly.

"So you didn't want anyone to know you were coming," I said, and James's silence confirmed it. I sighed. "It's all right. I understand."

"Why are you two out in the middle of the night?" James asked, switching to the offensive.

"We're going away for a bit," I said.

"What? Where? Why?"

"It doesn't matter," Anders replied.

"Yes, it does. Please, tell me."

I didn't know how to tell James the least amount of satisfactory information so that we could continue, unquestioned any further. "There will be a blood moon here in several months. As a Hersote, I believe it may impact me. So Anders and I are going to go find an island where we might find a practice blood moon of sorts," I tried, afraid that this explanation would actually create more questions than it quelled.

"A practice—what? Where is it?"

"We're not sure," Anders said. "But we really must be going. We'd like to leave unnoticed if you don't mind."

"Well...," James began, pausing for what seemed an eternity, "let me come with you!"

"What? Why?" I said.

"As an apology, for not coming to your side when everything happened with Celia, and then at the funeral," James trailed off.

"You don't have to do that," Anders stated strongly.

"Please, let me. I want to help you both. Just—just let me do a couple of things."

"I'm sorry, James, but we're leaving now," I stated firmly.

"Where are you going first?"

I waited a beat before grudgingly answering, "Ballos Port."

"All right. Give me an hour after you arrive," he stated without hesitation. "Then feel free to continue on to wherever you need to go if I don't find you. But just give me an hour. I want to help you do whatever it is you need to do."

Anders sighed loudly. "Fine. One hour."

"See you soon," James said, and I heard his feet thudding loudly on the dirt as he turned the corner and ran off. Coming out quietly to the front of my house, we could see his dark figure, running down the road toward his house. We turned in the opposite direction, toward the empty fields before us.

Out of the shadows, I could make out Anders' features a bit better, but still in no detail. "Are we actually waiting an hour for James and letting him come with us?" I asked.

Anders shook his head exasperatedly. "I don't know. I don't think he'll actually show up. I really like James, but he's not exactly the leave on a second's notice kind of guy. And going against public opinion and supporting us isn't exactly his strong suit either."

"But if he does show up?" I asked.

"Then I suppose we'll let him come with us. Can't hurt to have another friend with us," Anders said. "Though I really don't think we'll see him again until after we return."

Chapter Six

"You've got to be kidding me," Anders said, gazing out at the road coming into Ballos Port from our village. Not only was James's short light brown hair and deceivingly muscular arms swinging at his sides visible in the distance, but he was surrounded by what appeared to be the rest of our group of friends.

"What do we do?" I asked quickly, glancing at Anders in panic. Were they here to help or hinder us in our mission, I wondered. James had seemed genuine enough, but I thought I could make out Raela's medium brown hair standing out lighter than usual against a solid black dress; I was not anxious to see her again so soon after Celia's funeral.

"I—I guess we just see what they want," Anders replied, checking our surroundings as he spoke. We were standing at the edge of the port, the sun having just broken over the horizon not twenty minutes before. The port was already busy with people loading supplies into boats, and the stone shops across the street were beginning to show signs of life as shopkeepers swung open windows or brushed off front stoops.

"They can't attack us. There are too many people around," Anders said, shifting his weight and clenching his fists at his sides nonetheless.

"Is that what they're thinking about?" I asked, panicked.

"You know I'm not a mind reader," Anders said a bit too harshly under the stress of our unexpected situation.

"Well are they afraid of anything?" I asked. They were growing closer, and I could now make out the features of all of our friends, even Gregory.

Anders looked tense for a moment, but then I saw the muscles around his jaw relax and his fists half unclench. "I think it will be all right," he said, and he gave a hesitant, friendly wave as our friends approached.

"I'm glad you're still here," James said, leading the group, a position I could not think of seeing him in at any other point in time.

"Well, you were here within an hour," I said, giving a nervous little laugh. James looked happy, but unusually intense, his blue eyes focused on Anders and mine in turn as if we were engaged in a heated debate.

Agatha looked nervous, her mousy brown hair falling across her face as she kept her gaze primarily on her tiny feet. Gregory, for once, was not staring at Agatha, ready to support her every step. Instead he stood with his own arms crossed and his feet planted firmly on the ground, surveying Anders and I with an uncomfortable appraisal of superiority, his nostrils flared and his head tilted upward just slightly. Meanwhile, Darius's massive body seemed contrastingly calm, his noticeably muscular arms hanging limply at his sides and his thick neck relaxed as his shoulders were comfortably slumped. The small half-smile on his mouth was somewhat reassuring, after having rested my eyes first on Gregory. And then there was Raela, her perfect hourglass figure shown off nicely in the tight black mourning dress she was wearing, her hair down, quite out of character. Unlike her younger sister from the day before, her body looked limp and powerless, her shoulders somewhat hunched and her cheeks void of color as her green eyes looked into my solid blue ones, at times seeming to swim out of focus.

"So," Anders said, seemingly unconsciously moving a hair closer to me so that the sides of our arms grazed each other, "we didn't expect to see you all here."

"Well," James said, again taking on the unusual leadership role, "I wanted to give the others a fair chance to make amends with you too."

"We're all very sorry," Darius spoke up. "We should have come to your side. It just—it was all a shock. Not that we should have cut you so harshly out of our group during such a hard time. So…we're sorry."

"It's all right," I said quietly, cracking the hint of a smile, which I focused on Darius's friendliest face. I saw Anders nod in agreement out of the corner of my eye.

"So," James began again, glancing at our friends around him awkwardly, as if he had just realized that he was taking on an unwanted role as ambassador for the group, "I told everyone what you told me about the blood moon, and the others were thinking of helping too."

"Oh?" I said, a bit surprised as I glanced at Raela's black dress and Agatha's hair-shielded face.

"But first we wanted to know the truth from you. What is going on?"

Gregory demanded, his voice coming out louder than James's had been.

"All right," I said slowly, drawing out the vowels in uncertainty. "Well, I guess—wait. First, no one at home knows where we are, right?"

"I left a note simply saying that we were all right, but had gone away for a time," James said. I wondered if people would think that the evil Hersote had done away with them, but that was something I had no control over at that point.

"Well," I began again, "I should probably start at the beginning." And for the second time in less than twelve hours, I told the horrific story of my mother's death.

"So, I'd like to go and see it in preparation for the coming blood moon," I finished awkwardly. A seagull laughed loudly close at hand, and the air carried the heavy scent of fresh fish as a recently docked boat on the pier closest to us unloaded its bountiful catch.

"Well, will it be dangerous to be around you?" James asked, his straight eyebrows raised in concerned question.

"I'm not sure, which is why I'm not expecting any of you to go," I said.

"Well why is Anders going?" Gregory asked suspiciously. "Does he have this power too?"

I had purposefully left out Anders' own identity as a Slyton in the telling of my tale and his reason for wishing to visit the island. It was his secret to tell if he chose, not mine. And he could better read the fears and concerns of our friends than I could.

I looked at Anders, his features calm and the hint of a smile on his lips. His words surprised me then. "I have secrets of my own, which I do not wish to share just yet. However, I am going partly to help Sarah in her own search."

"You can't possibly think we would go with you not knowing what you're up to," Gregory stated, and Agatha's curtain of hair became longer as her head bowed deeper.

"You don't need to come with us," Anders said casually.

"Will you ever tell us your secrets?" Darius asked gently.

Anders sighed and seemed to lose some of the purposefully casual tone he had embraced. "I think so, Darius. Just—give me a bit of time."

Darius nodded understandingly.

"So, if we do decide to go with you," Darius said, "you don't know anything about the island other than it took just over a week to travel to and it's somewhere in the west?"

"Yes," I replied unenthusiastically.

"But we thought that we would ask around here. Maybe someone knows something about it," Anders replied, much more energetically.

"There's no need to do that." The voice was Raela's and it took me by complete surprise to hear her speak. She had seemed almost like a statue the whole time, her skin like lifeless marble and her brown hair like a silky piece of fabric blowing in the breeze. "I know what the island is called," she said, and I could feel all of our eyes turning toward her in shock.

She took a deep, forced breath, as if recalling herself to life. "It's called Merendinappa Island. It's where the Hersote leaders came together and enacted the series of spells that made them into immortals. They ruled there for a time before moving on when they decided they wanted more space."

It was everyone else's turn to assume the demeanor of statues. How did she know this, I wondered, too confused to actually bring myself to speak the words.

We must have all looked quite comical, staring at Raela in confused shock, for a tiny smile actually escaped as she explained, "Part of applying and auditioning for the Court at Harpson is the singing of a loralyr, which is a traditional song that tells of history or a legend. I happened to choose one about Merendinappa Island. Celia had chosen one about King Theodore the Third, the founder of Harpson." She finished solemnly at mention of her twin sister.

"All right then," I finally said, breaking the short silence that followed Raela's explanation. "I suppose our next step is to find someone who can take us to Meradin...." I trailed off.

"Merendinappa Island," Raela finished for me.

"Thanks," I said, and Raela threw me the hint of another small smile.

"Well then," Anders said, a smile forming on his own mouth and his hands coming together in budding excitement, "are you coming with us or not?"

"Of course," James spoke first, actually taking another, friendly step toward us.

Darius nodded his head and Raela surprised me by actually saying, "Yes."

"Well, let's go find a boat then," I said, actually growing excited before Gregory's still-serious voice stopped me before I took a step.

"Sorry, but Agatha and I aren't going," he said.

"What?" I said, caught off guard.

"I'm very sorry, but we have a lot to do—our lives in Harpson and the coming wedding. We wish you all the best, though, and we won't tell anyone back in the village where you've gone since you seem to have wanted it a secret," Gregory said. He then stepped forward and strongly took Anders' hand and gave it a firm shake. He then nodded his head at me as a sort of parting signal, and he took Agatha's hand and swung her around, the two of them walking quickly down the road from whence they had come.

"Agatha never even said a word to us," I said in shock as we all looked after the two of them.

"They're still afraid of us, perhaps even more so after you told them about the island," Anders spoke distractedly.

"I'm sure that's not it," James said, trying to rally us despite the stiff parting. "They just have a bit more going on than arguably the rest of us have, I guess. I mean, obviously not all of us," he over-explained awkwardly, glancing at Raela who did not complete his eye contact.

"Well, let's find that boat," Darius said, the first to overcome our shock at the sudden departure of one of our best friends and the fiancé we had all embraced so openly.

As we started to walk further into the heart of Barros Port, I noticed that James had lost some of his confident bravado and Anders his excitement. I wondered if they were lamenting the further fracture of our group, for I knew I was.

Chapter Seven

The first two days passed on the small boat we had rented in tense near-silence. As the bottom of the deck was fairly cramped and windowless, we all spent a good portion of our time simply standing above deck, watching the crashing waves as we passed the very occasional island. The two-man crew went about their business dutifully, and while they talked loudly and tastelessly together, usually reminiscing about some port they had stopped at and what sort of women they had encountered there, they very rarely talked with the rest of us. Their sleeping quarters were separate from ours, adjacent to the cargo area, while we had the larger portion of the bottom of the boat, all sleeping beside each other, an unusual addition of intimacy to our recovering friendships.

In the middle of the third day, I was leaning against the front of the boat, the water particularly still and our boat seemingly making slow progress as we passed what looked like a tiny, uninhabited island.

I heard steps behind me and was a bit surprised to see Raela come up beside me and copy my casual stance of quiet contemplation. Out of the corner of my eye I saw her tuck her brown hair behind her ear on the side closest me, her lips pursed just slightly. "I really am sorry, you know," she spoke quietly, her gaze still focused on the sea.

"It's all right," I said, turning to look at her and noticing a silent tear rolling down her cheek. "I'm sorry I couldn't save her."

Raela broke into a subdued sob before finally saying, "I know." She brushed her cheeks dry with the back of her hand and finally made eye contact as she choked out through a forced smile, "So, are you nervous about going to Merendinappa Island again?"

"A bit. I guess I'm trying not to think about it," I said.

"I understand. I—I can't imagine carrying that burden around. I don't know how you've done it."

I half-snorted. "I don't know either. But, hopefully I figure out if I'll be a danger to anyone before the actual blood moon occurs."

"Yea," she agreed. "So…if you don't mind me asking…what sort of magic do you have?"

"I don't know actually. After the accident with my mother, I never wanted to have anything to do with magic," I answered.

She nodded her head, her jaw tightened. "I understand."

"So, are you still going to go to Harpson?" I asked after a minute.

"I plan to do so, yes. But they'll have to excuse me a small period of bereavement. I just—I'm doing this to help you, but part of me was very happy for the excuse to just get away for a time."

"I understand," it was my turn to say.

Another brief pause followed before Raela asked, "You aren't worried about sunburn?"

I looked at my warm, milky white skin. "Honestly, I hadn't given it much thought."

"Wait here, I bought some sun protectant at Barros Port," and she ran off to the stairs at the back of the boat, leading to the lower level. She was back in a minute, offering me a bit of cream from a glass jar.

"Thanks," I accepted, spreading a bit of it across my arms and onto my nose.

"You're welcome. I burn so easily, I wear it constantly."

"I know. You always smell good from it, like flowers," I said.

She genuinely smiled. "Well thanks."

"Where are the guys?" I said, beginning to feel truly relaxed for the first time in days. It was then that I realized we were being watched, quite intently, by our three other friends, all from different spots on the deck.

"I think they were maybe waiting to take a cue from us," I whispered conspiratorially to Raela.

She nodded and smiled at me knowingly and began signaling each of them over. They all walked our way, almost suspiciously.

"Don't just stand there staring at us. Come over and talk to us," I said as they drew nearer.

"We didn't want to interrupt," James voiced awkwardly.

"We're still all friends," Raela said kindly. "We might as well act like it." And the five of us stood on the deck, breathing in the calm salt air.

We all ate under the setting sun that night, reclining on the deck of that boat like we had at our picnic on the grassy hill. Our group was noticeably smaller, but once again breathed with life. As the stars came out above us, James lectured us all on the various constellations.

Eventually, with some reluctance, Raela excused herself from the group, her eyelids noticeably heavy with sleep in the starlit night. Soon afterward, James and Darius both excused themselves, leaving me alone with Anders.

He was completely reclined on the deck, looking up at the stars, and I sat a couple of feet away, my legs bent in front of me, holding myself into a backward, semi-reclined position with my hands.

"So, you're not going to kiss me too, are you?" Anders asked mischievously, and it took me several seconds to realize that he was drawing a clumsy comparison to the night I had been left alone at the lake with James.

"Don't count on it," I said, smirking up at the stars.

"Of course not," Anders said, just a bit too seriously. I glanced at his face to examine it for signs of joking when he continued abruptly, "Mrs. Lindle approached my mother with a marriage contract last week."

"She—what?" I asked, completely caught off guard.

"For Emily, of course," he said, keeping his eyes firmly on the stars above.

"Right," I said slowly. "Did your parents accept it?" I asked.

He laughed through his nose, not quite a snort. "No. They told me about it in case I wanted to accept, but how could I? Emily will die. I won't. Eventually she'd realize I wasn't getting any older. And what then? Fake my own death in a few years so that my own wife wouldn't fear me if she realized what I was? Though I guess all of that's changed now that the entire village knows I'm immortal."

"Did you want to marry Emily?" I asked hesitantly, afraid I might upset him.

"I—I don't know. I barely know the girl. She's very pretty, but fairly young, and the idea of Mrs. Lindle as a mother-in-law." I could almost hear the eye roll in his voice.

"My parents each found an immortal partner, which is what I suppose I will have to do one day," he continued. "But I've always hated that—being so limited in my choice to love. I always," he cut himself off with a deep breath as he brushed a hand over his face. "I always pictured finding a beautiful mortal girl," he continued. "And together we would go on fantastic and dangerous adventures, looking for a way to make her immortal too, so that we could be together always. We would be fighting against the odds, but we would do it, and so we could live our days together forever." He sat up and looked at me sheepishly, his cheeks noticeably red under the night's twinkling lights. "Just a silly fantasy I had from years back."

I threw him what I hoped was a comforting smile, though I truly couldn't completely relate. After my childhood experience on the island, I had never longed for great adventure, and I had never considered the differences between finding an immortal or a mortal partner. My parents, after all, had had a most unique marriage. I assumed I would figure it out when the right person walked into my life. Perhaps, though, planning was necessary, as Anders inadvertently pointed out.

"Sorry," Anders said, interrupting my private thoughts. "I didn't mean to stress you out."

"No, no. It's fine," I said, realizing that he must have been able to sense my fears about the unknowns and complications surrounding an immortal finding a suitable partner.

"How about we go to sleep?" he said.

"All right," I agreed, and we stood and made our way to the stairs and our sleeping quarters.

As we descended the stairs, singing could be heard floating up from below. Raela's beautiful voice was creating a slow, deep tune, made almost haunting by the flickering candlelight below as she came into view. She was sitting upright in the corner as Darius and James lay reclined near her feet, listening to her sweet voice. I sat down on my own pile of blankets before realizing that she was singing the song she must have learned for the Court at Harpson about Merendinappa Island.

And in turns they talked and whispered how
Their lifeblood would flow and never fail
Never in death would they say goodbye
And they sent their words into the sky

The breeze blows magic at Merendinappa
The magic trickles through the palm trees
The flowers bloom bright at Merendinappa
They will never wilt or fade

For life was born at Merendinappa
Life for those who would die

When she finished there was hushed silence.

"That was beautiful," James said quietly. "Please, sing one more. How about Town Square Song?" he asked.

"All right, but it won't sound like it usually does," she said. I was confused at her meaning until she opened her mouth and started to sing. The words were the same, about a young girl who gazes at her love everyday across the town square, but the tune was completely different. Raela's beautiful voice was smooth and tried to fill in a deeper version of the melody, though it became a painful reminder that Celia always carried the higher melody. And while the two sisters were almost never found apart, Raela would from then on have to try to fill in the melody of those songs that had at one time been effortless beauty.

Chapter Eight

A week and a half after we had left Barros Port, we found ourselves standing on that hauntingly familiar white sand beach from my childhood. It was almost exactly how I remembered it and how I still dreamt about it on my more troubled nights.

"Does it look the same?" Anders asked me gently as we all stood staring at the massive wall before us, the two crew members remaining on deck.

"Yes," I said, my mouth dry and sticky. "All right," I said, taking a breath as I collected my thoughts and my nerve. "We know what we're all doing. I'll go through and to the top first. I'm fairly certain everything will go away once I step off of the stone that seemed to make the blood moon appear to me. We'll go with just that simple step first. You guys wait on this side of the gate, and when I come back, let me know if you saw the blood moon or not." I took another deep breath. "One step at a time," I said, largely trying to reassure myself.

"Well, first we have to find the opening. Do you know where it is?" Anders asked, indicating the tangle of vines covering the wall before us.

"It's somewhere in the middle. I'll just go through feeling points on the stone. That's how I found it last time."

And so the five of us walked forward, the others pulling back portions of the vines as they were able in search of a door, me just blindly thrusting my hand through to the cold stone.

Ten minutes into our search, I still hadn't found the door when Darius shouted, "I think I might have found something."

All five of us ran over to him, where he was holding back a clump of vines to reveal a carved picture of a key.

"Let's give it a try shall we?" I said quickly, my nerves creating a lump in my throat. I reached out and touched the key, and at once a doorway began to open, snapping the vines around it as it had for me years before.

Ahead of us was the same perfect path of my memories, and the same brilliant flowers at least a foot in diameter.

"Can we just look at the inside of the path for a minute before you go to the top?" Raela asked breathlessly. I shook just looking at it, but I found my mouth acquiesced to her request.

We stood in a little clump just on the other side of the Gate of Wrotins, staring at the oversized flowers surrounding the dirt path. "I can't believe how taken care of this place looks," Raela said, reminding me of the comments of the adults on my previous visit to the island.

"All right," I said, cutting into the apparent awe of the others, "I'm going to go on and find the blood moon at the top of the hill."

And all at once, I felt my joints stiffen into stone. My eyes swiveled in my frozen head, unable to turn to look behind me, my view stuck instead on the completely still figures of my friends. Their own eyes darted about wildly in contrast to their frozen expressions of simple interest, with normally leveled eyebrows and mildly parted lips.

"You're not going to the top of this hill," a measured voice said, and though I couldn't look in its direction as I was staring at my friends, I saw all of their eyes glance in its direction to their right.

Several seconds later, the person who had spoken stepped right in front of me. She was of a nearly identical height to my own, so I was able to look straight into her pale blue eyes. "Clara," she said, breaking eye contact for a moment and looking behind me, "release this girl's mouth." A strange melting sensation invaded my jaw, leaving it tingling and shaking momentarily.

"Who are you?" the first woman demanded, staring once more into my eyes.

"No, who are you?" I shot at her, my apparent bravery not matching the serious physical predicament in which I found myself.

She smiled, almost kindly. "My name is Verdenia. I'm a Hersote, and I'm here to protect this area from you. Searching for a blood moon? I'm sure the Hersote leaders will be very interested to meet you. See you in a few days," she said, and she pushed something invisible in my direction.

Chapter Nine

It felt as if I had just been on the island the second before, staring at the intimidating Hersote, Verdenia. But seemingly in the blink of an eye, I found myself reclined in a dim, creaking environment, my joints frozen in a sleeping position on my side. Between the small, rhythmic creaking and the sound of tiny waves outside, it didn't take me long to realize that I was in the hold of a boat. Were it not for my immobile joints, I might have thought I had dreamt of arriving at Merendinappa Island.

While I was simply staring at the planks on the inside of the boat's wall, my view quickly changed as a shadowed face knelt down, only inches from my own.

"Don't think about trying anything tricky," Verdenia warned sternly, her features obscured by the lack of light below deck.

"Where are my friends?" I asked at once.

"They're right behind you, and they will remain safe if you cooperate," she said, pushing herself upright and walking away, her footfalls and what sounded like a second set clunking loudly on wooden steps somewhere.

"Anders? Raela? You there?" I called after a minute. There was no answer. "James? Darius?" Still no response.

I waited perhaps a full hour in immobile silence, unable to turn and see if Verdenia had been truthful in telling me that my friends were right behind me. Finally, though, I heard loud talking above deck, which grew louder as a group of people noisily descended the stairs breaking the dimness with the arrival of what I assumed were lanterns.

I could hear them shuffling around near my feet, though I couldn't see them with my neck frozen in place. I was struggling to make out specific sentences when all at once the talking stopped.

"Sarah, we are going to unfreeze you and your companions," a calm, deeper womanly voice announced. "It is my sincere hope that your attempt to find the blood moon was merely misguided confusion and not an attempt to harm your own people. That being said, I have many powerful Hersotes here with me if you do indeed mean us harm. So, if you would like to remain free and you would like your friends to live, if they are indeed mortal, then I suggest cooperating and not trying to fight us."

A few seconds passed after this elaborate threat when I felt my joints loosen in a fluid, melting motion. I turned onto my stomach and went to push myself up with my hands, though fell awkwardly onto my face when my strength failed me.

"Take your time," the same measured, stern voice said. "Ruth's talents lie in sleep and unconsciousness. She's had you asleep for a few days while you made your way here, so your body may be a tiny bit weak, but you should feel back to normal in a minute."

I took a deep breath and pushed myself up once more, this time into a successful seated position. There appeared to be at least a dozen people below deck with us, but I gave them no scrutiny as I turned my head to check on my friends. They were all there, Darius right next to me, seated like I was, Raela in the process of doing so, and Anders and James already standing.

"Sorry we didn't answer you when you called," Darius said to me quietly the second our eyes locked. "My mouth was frozen, and I assume the others' were too."

I nodded in comprehension and looked back at the group assembled before us. No one was standing in a position of prominence, so I was not sure who had been the vocal one. The group was made up of men and women, and it was then that I realized that I had never met, at least knowingly, a male Hersote. Like most of the women, their hair was lighter in color, though cut much shorter, the longest falling to just above his shoulders. They also seemed tall, the shortest man still taller than most of the women.

While none of the men and women were particularly overweight, their slenderness did vary slightly, though more with apparent build than fat. I was surprised to see a couple who looked to be the age of grandparents, though most of them appeared to be perhaps in their mid-twenties, with clearly adult faces, but free of any wrinkles or creases, their eyes all brightly reflecting the lanterns a few of them had brought.

Finally, that same female voice spoke, and it was the woman directly in front of me. "Am I correct in my assumption that you are Sarah, daughter of Florence?"

Though not old, she was older than what I understood most Hersotes to be, perhaps in her early forties, the faintest signs of wrinkles in her hands and her facial skin just not quite as taut as her younger companions'.

"I am," I said, holding her intense eye contact, her green eyes glimmering like emeralds.

"And do you mean us harm?" she asked.

"No."

There was a very slight shift in the movement of the group at my answer.

"And so why were you looking for a blood moon at Merendinappa?" she asked, a hint of suspicion present in her voice.

I considered lying, but could see no harm in relaying the truth, and so I continued. "As a young child, I visited with my mother. But a blood moon appeared to me while I was there, immediately preceding the death of my immortal mother. It was something I do not wish to accidentally repeat when there is a blood moon a few months from now, so I went in search of the one I saw as a child, hoping to learn more about it."

There was another small shift in the group in front of me, a few of them actually starting to wear cautious smiles, only slightly upturned, and mostly portrayed by the widening of their eyes.

"I see," the same woman spoke, carefully scrutinizing my face, presumably for signs of lying and deceit. "But you did successfully kill Florence Rengla?" she asked, using my mother's maiden name.

"I think an awful accident such as what I lived through with my own mother can hardly be referred to as successful," I said sternly. The smiles on the few faces had disappeared after this woman's question and mention of my mother's death, but they reappeared after my impassioned rebuttal.

"I understand," the woman said calmly. "And may I ask what type of magic you have?"

"I don't know."

"What do you mean you don't know?" the woman asked, confusion breaking through her calm façade of complete control and understanding.

"After I believe I accidentally used magic to end my mother's life, I wanted nothing to do with it. I never learned."

A couple of people in the group actually began whispering to each other as the spokeswoman finally wore a tiny smile of her own. "Very well," she said, her voice a bit higher and friendlier in tone. "It seems that this is all a misunderstanding then. Please, let's go above deck where we may talk more freely and pleasantly," and she made a gesture indicating that my friends and I should lead the way.

Though farthest from the stairs, I went first, my friends following silently behind me.

Outside, I used my arm to shield my eyes from the bright sun. On this cloudless day, it took a while for my eyes to adjust so I could see that the boat we were on, which was not the same as the one we had used for travel to Merendinappa, was docked at a well-maintained port. Before us, brightly reflecting the sun's rays, stood hundreds of buildings of bright white stone, rising and falling with the gentle dips in the land before us.

While we silently stared at the impressive scene, the Hersotes crowded around us on the deck. Finally, the woman who kept speaking announced from behind us, "Welcome to Grotania, current home of the Hersotes." She carefully pushed her way past me so that she was facing us. "My name, by the way, is Octavia. I'm one of the Twelve here."

"Twelve what?" Darius asked skeptically, clearly unimpressed by the woman's announcement.

Octavia actually laughed slightly before answering, as if Darius had asked a very stupid question. "The twelve royal leaders here. Part of the group that came to rule the Hersotes after we discovered the secret to immortality."

"You mean you're one of the people who actually cast the spell that made the Hersotes immortal?" James asked in awe, his enthusiasm in sharp contrast to Darius's question.

"Yes. We all gathered at Merendinappa Island, where you presumably saw your blood moon," she said, nodding her head briefly at me. "We then each contributed our part of the spell."

"What did you contribute?" Raela asked cautiously.

Octavia smiled and stood just a little straighter. "Health. I've always had a very powerful ability to help people overcome illnesses. It's been a most important ingredient in enjoying our immortality, not weighed down by normal human illnesses." She smiled at our group and then abruptly continued, "Shall we take you on a tour?" She marched ahead without waiting for an answer, her blonde hair flying loose and free in the sea breeze. Our whole group silently followed as the crowd of Hersotes energetically walked with us.

"This is our Florience Port," Octavia began with a wave at our surroundings. "It was one of the first things constructed when we moved here about a thousand years ago." The fresh wood and glistening waterproofing looked brand new, and I wondered if it were regularly replaced or preserved with magic, as Merendinappa Island was.

Moving off the wooden docks, we made our way to what appeared to be a main thoroughfare, the cobblestones smooth and inviting, the buildings on either side spotless and shining. Here and there the occasional Hersote stood or walked, coming to a complete stop at the sight of us and staring with unabashed interest.

"Here is our market," Octavia said, gesturing to a large, two-story building on the right. "There is also a courtyard on the other side where we have greenhouses that grow the tastiest produce and most beautiful flowers in the world."

Less than a minute away, she gestured to the left side of the street. "And this is Eliona's, in my opinion the most beautiful and wonderful restaurant in all of Grotania." The white building itself was probably only the size of my own modest home, though the outside area around it was at least five times the size, filled with green garlands, climbing vines with pink flowers, and honeysuckle bushes all along the perimeter, filling the air with its sweet scents. Tables were distributed throughout the greenery, and a few were occupied at that moment, its customers turning to look at us with an intensity that most would have found rude.

"What if it rains?" Anders asked. "There doesn't appear to be much inside seating."

Octavia laughed slightly. "You mortals amuse me with your limited minds," she said. Our group exchanged very slight looks, as we all knew that Anders was immortal, even if the others didn't know his true identity. Still, we remained quiet as Octavia continued, not sparing a glance for us. "It never rains on the square at Eliona's. We have magic for things like that."

Octavia made a right turn at the end of the street. "Here is Gregoria's, another restaurant," she said.

"A better restaurant," a man to our left piped up playfully.

"You young people," Octavia said with a flip of her hand, dismissing the man who appeared perhaps twenty years of age, and I wondered if he were really that young.

In contrast to Eliona's, Gregoria's was an intimidating stone structure four stories high, the outside decorated with thick marble columns that would take all five of us holding hands to wrap around one.

"And on our right is our music hall," Octavia continued. This structure was shorter than Gregoria's at only three stories, but it was much longer, running half the length of the entire street, its giant double doors shining with gold.

"Raela's a singer," James said, clearly trying to be friendly and break some of the subdued demeanor among our group.

"Fascinating," Octavia said flatly. "The singers and musicians at our music hall have been honing their skills for at least a century each."

I glanced at Raela whose slender nose flattened just slightly as her nostrils flared.

"What's that at the end of the street?" Darius asked, indicating the building where the street ended and forced a change in direction.

"Oh, just a home for one of our community members," Octavia said dismissively. Upon reaching it, we continued left down the next street, though I couldn't help but stare at this supposed residence. Many of the houses were blinding in the bright sun, but the building at the end of the street seemed to actually give off a faint glow. I wondered what kind of magic must be causing this, but I kept walking with the group as Octavia pointed out a gallery to the left on this new street.

This tour lasted over an hour, with limited talking on our part. "And here we have reached our residential quarters," Octavia announced. The houses were very similar here, built with the same white stone found everywhere else. "And this is where you can stay," she continued, pointing to a thin, three-story building with a simple green hedge out front.

"Where we can stay?" I repeated.

"Of course," Octavia continued calmly, finally turning to look at us. "I assume you'll have questions for us about your experience with the blood moon, and I can't imagine you'd want to return home so soon."

"Oh," I said, having not thought to simply ask the Hersotes here about the blood moon. "All right," I hesitantly accepted, looking into the eyes of my equally as hesitant friends.

"Wonderful," Octavia said, stepping to the side and outstretching her arm in the direction of the front door. "Sylvia is inside to help you feel comfortable during your stay here. We have business to attend to now, but I'll schedule some more time to meet with you in three days."

"Three days?" Anders asked, clearly unhappy about the time table.

"Oh, I always forget that three days must seem like an eternity to mortals. But don't worry. It will be here before you know it," Octavia said, and without further remarks, she walked past us and back down the street toward the commercial district, the group of Hersotes following.

We waited there in the street in front of this house as they disappeared. "Well, should we go in?" I finally asked my friends. James was the only one to respond with a partial shrug of acceptance. I led the way to the front door, noticing a curious face staring at us through a window at the next house down.

The door was made of smooth cherry red wood, the white exterior spotless.

Opening the door, we looked in on an overlarge eat-in kitchen.

"Welcome!" a young woman greeted us as we stepped over the threshold. Her light brown hair was tied up in a bun and although she wore a tight, pretty green cotton dress, it was covered by a simple black apron. "My name is Sylvia. I'll be staying with you all during your stay. Please, feel free to ask me for anything you need."

"Thank you, Sylvia," I accepted awkwardly. She looked perhaps our age, though she obviously could have been hundreds of years old.

"I've just finished preparing your supper," she said, indicating a boiling pot on the stove. "Crushed lentilla nut and squash soup. I do hope you like it," she said, and she hurried over to the stove where she began pouring the soup into bowls. My friends looked silently at me for direction, and I nodded toward the table where we each wordlessly took a seat as Sylvia began bringing us porcelain bowls filled with the soup.

"It smells delicious," I said, and my voice sounded loud in the quiet of the house.

"I'm so glad you think so," Sylvia said, smiling brightly, her blue eyes catching the light from the many open windows on this floor.

Once the last of us was served, we all started eating in silence. "Tastes delicious too," I said after the first gulp of the smooth, nutty soup, and my friends agreed.

"I'm so glad you like it," Sylvia responded eagerly, and she simply stood in the corner staring at us as we continued eating.

After a few minutes, I was eager to break the strange silence and the intense and ever-watchful eye of Sylvia. "So Sylvia," I began in as friendly a tone as possible, "how did you ever find yourself stuck with the job of waiting on us while we're here?" I smiled at her, hoping I was encouraging camaraderie rather than being insulting.

"Oh, it's a wonderful honor, I can assure you," she said brightly. "Though it is true that I was an easy choice as I don't yet have a true skill or other place of business. You see, I'm the youngest here in Grotania."

"So what, you're only 340?" Darius asked, his eyes focused on his soup.

Sylvia laughed pleasantly, the sound melodic and high-pitched. "Hardly. I actually am quite young at only twenty years old."

"Oh wow. You're really about our age then," I said, genuinely surprised.

"How old is the second youngest person here?" James asked, seeming genuinely interested.

"112, I believe," she answered without hesitation.

"And you're immortal?" I asked, and I noticed Raela look at me with a confused cock of her head.

"Oh, yes," Sylvia answered.

"I thought all Hersotes are immortal," Raela said.

"Not necessarily," I replied. "Half-Hersotes can be mortal."

"This is true," Sylvia confirmed. "Though you won't find any half-Hersotes here."

"I'm actually a half-Hersote," I said before taking another spoonful of soup.

"Really?" Sylvia asked, her blue eyes unblinkingly focused on me. "Is your father or your mother a Hersote?"

"My mother," I answered.

"Fascinating," she said, unconsciously taking an excited step toward our table. "And what was your father?"

"A Lellio," I answered.

"Well that's the next best thing, I suppose," Sylvia said seriously, though she then looked uncomfortably at my friends. "No disrespect intended if you are something different," she added sheepishly.

"None taken," James accepted graciously.

"We're Losos," Darius simply stated.

"I see. Hill or sea people?" Sylvia asked, quickly attempting to seem equally interested in their heritage as she had been in mine.

"Hill," Darius answered.

"Wonderful," Sylvia said.

Anders didn't offer his true identity, which I thought was wise. I certainly didn't yet trust these Hersotes, and the silence from my friends as to Anders' immortal status told me they felt likewise.

"So, if you don't mind me asking, why are you here?" Sylvia asked, obviously eager to keep the conversation going. "I was only just summoned. There is a town meeting being held tonight to discuss how to make you feel most welcome here, but until then, we're all kind of in the dark."

"Oh, we, um, ran into some Hersotes while visiting Merendinappa Island," I said uneasily.

"Really? I have never been to Merendinappa Island. You know we're forbidden to go there without a specific purpose?"

"Really? Why?" I asked, halfway through my soup.

"Well, the magic that was performed there is quite powerful. I suppose some of it still lingers and could prove dangerous if accidentally tangled with."

"Yes...I suppose so." I took another several gulps of soup before asking, "Sylvia, on the way here we passed a building that seemed to glow, over by the music hall."

"Oh, you mean the Confinement?" she asked.

"What is it?" My friends all stopped eating to look at her as she answered.

"The Confinement. It's where they keep Meraldia."

"Who's Meraldia?" Anders asked.

"Oh, it's a scandalous, awful tale," Sylvia said, her voice lowering in tone as she spoke in a hush.

I indicated one of the several empty extra seats around the table, and Sylvia scampered to it and sat down happily. "Meraldia was one of the Twelve," she continued the second she was seated. She held a strange power, rare. It was cyclical in nature. Like she had some control over waves when at the shore, or she was able to help a heart keep beating steady and strong while a person was in physical distress. So when the immortality spell was performed she was able to make it so that our hearts keep beating regularly and our lungs never tire." Sylvia was practically whispering for dramatic effect.

"But then, it was discovered that in her selfishness Meraldia had added a secret piece to the immortality spell, one that would undo what the Twelve worked so hard to accomplish—a piece that breaks the cycle. However, she needs to be out of the Confinement and freed in order to enact it. And so that's why she is forever imprisoned there. The glow you see is from the magic keeping her safely contained, and there are always a couple of Hersotes guarding her too."

"Wow," I said. "That's really fascinating."

"It is, isn't it?" Sylvia said, and with a quick, somewhat horrified look at Darius's empty bowl, she sprang from her chair. "Can I bring you some more soup?" she asked.

"No, I'm full, thank you," Darius said, just a bit warmer than he had been.

After we each finished our meals, Sylvia took us to the other levels of the house. "This floor houses enough beds for the men," she said, and I saw that the spacious room was divided into four separate sleeping sections with no enclosed divisions.

Climbing the next set of stairs we arrived in a sitting room of sorts, a long cushioned sofa of white placed along the side wall. A large maroon rug covered most of the hard stone floor, and a small, low table stood in the center of the room. Several candle holders were attached to the walls, and a center candelabra hung from the ceiling. A painted picture of the sea and a sunrise or sunset hung above the sofa, its main colors orange and pink. "And here is the sitting room, for use for both genders. And over here," she continued, walking toward a door on this floor, "is where the ladies may sleep." We each peeked inside where two beds had been made up on opposite sides of the room.

"And finally," Sylvia said, indicating a thin, unobtrusive flight of stairs at the far wall in the sitting room, "you may also use the roof to recline and relax, though there is currently no furniture up there for doing so."

"Wonderful, thank you," I said.

Thankfully, Sylvia made a natural exit at this point. "Well, I'll let you all settle in. I have some cleaning to do from the meal. Then I have to go to that meeting I told you about, but I'll be back after that. I'll be setting up a place to sleep in the kitchen, so if you need anything during the night, please don't hesitate to ask," she said.

As she began her descent to the first floor, James and Darius both made their way to the white sofa and plopped down onto it as Raela, Anders, and I faced them, sitting on the rug around the small table.

"So…this is all very strange, right?" Darius asked first.

"Very," Raela said, her eyebrows drawn down in apparent discomfort.

"Yes, though maybe it's a good thing," I said. "After all, in a few days we can meet with Octavia again and ask some questions about the blood moon."

"I don't trust them, though," Anders spoke up. "I mean, they kidnapped us. And with the exception of Sylvia they haven't exactly been friendly toward us. Hospitable, yes. Friendly, not quite. I can't really put my finger on it."

"I can't say I trust them either," I said in hushed tones with a glance at the stairs. "But we might as well wait and meet with them for now."

"No, I agree," Anders said. "Something about their treatment of us just…creeps me out, I guess."

James was chewing on his bottom lip, listening intently to the conversation while Darius and Raela glanced around the room.

"So…this is where your mom grew up?" Anders asked.

"Yes. She was born after they would have left Merendinappa Island," I said, glancing out the closest window where we had a view of another house as tall as the one in which we were staying.

"Do you know if you have family here still?" Raela asked.

"I don't know that for sure, though I would assume I did. I think my mom left her own parents here when she moved off of this island."

"Did you want to ask about them and meet them if you do have grandparents here?" James questioned.

"I—I don't know. I hadn't given it any thought until now," I answered truthfully.

Raela yawned at my side then. The light was still streaming through the windows, but I found myself copying her yawn.

"Maybe we should get some rest," Darius said, stretching his arms high above his head. "I know we were asleep or what have you for a while apparently, but I'm still pretty tired."

"Me too," James agreed.

"All right then," I said, and I stood up first. "Good night guys."

Everyone repeated similar sentiments and Anders, James, and Darius headed back down the stairs while Raela and I turned into the bedroom on the third floor.

Chapter Ten

A bright beam of light lay across my eyes as I blinked them open. I assumed it was the morning sun, but quickly realized the light was too blue for that and the surrounding room too dark. My eyes quickly adjusting, I realized that it was intense moonlight breaking through the crack in the curtains. With a quick glance at the other bed, I saw that Raela was still sleeping. I stood and tiptoed to the curtain to draw it tighter, but not before peeking out into the night. The moon was quite large, currently growing fuller each night, but its light was made even brighter by the white buildings reflecting its cool light.

I shut the curtain and crawled back into bed and closed my eyes. I turned onto my side, trying to go back to sleep, but my strange surroundings seemed to echo discomfort to me, keeping me awake. I turned onto my other side, facing the door. It was then that I thought I heard the slightest noise coming from outside our bedroom door. I stood once more, the hard floor cool on my bare feet, and tiptoed to it. With my ear pressed against the door, I could make out muffled talking. Very, very slowly, I pressed down on the door handle and noiselessly pushed the door open a crack. The people talking did not seem to notice as they continued their hushed conversation. I was thankful, then, to recognize the whispers as those of James and Anders, and not some Hersote intruder. They were probably just using the common area to relax if Darius were asleep.

I was about to close the door and return to bed when I caught my own name among the whispers.

"I don't know. I just always liked how Sarah never seemed to have any fears, any misgivings. She was like this unusual rock of a woman. But now it seems that she does have fears, and she's just been hiding them all this time," James was whispering.

"Yea, but she's opened up to us about them now. And it's kind of natural to be afraid of some things," Anders replied.

"Well, yes, of course. But it's just such a huge jump from the person I thought she was. In my mind, she went from being totally fearless to having such complex fears that I don't really know how to be there for her except to offer my help as much as possible."

"How else would you like to be there for her?" Anders asked.

"I don't know. I just—I can't talk about her feelings or relate to her in any way now really. Her struggles are just so…overwhelming."

"I suppose," Anders said slowly. "But don't the bizarrely tragic things she's been through and the way she's handling them make her fascinating to you? Yes, she does feel fear, but she's still a strong woman, smart and kind even though she's direct. And she's not some bitter, miserable person. She loves dancing and music. And she loves the outdoors. She's complicated, but that just means we have the opportunity to dig in deeply and know her better, which is something I myself am only just starting to embrace. I've spent a lot of my time, honestly, trying to avoid her on any kind of deeper level, I suppose."

I held my breath, waiting for James to ask why, as this last comment almost demanded Anders giving up his own secret. Instead, James simply gave a drawn-out, "Yea," and I wondered if he had listened to a word Anders had just said or if he were stuck in his own thoughts.

One of them sighed deeply.

"I guess I just feel more comfortable around Raela and her types of fears and life experiences," James said. "Not that I want to abandon Sarah and this quest of sorts that we're on. I mean, I care about her. We've all been friends for forever. It's just," and I could almost hear the rambling and running of his mind. "Raela just lost her sister, and even though I don't have a sibling, those feelings of sadness are much more relatable to me than Sarah's. And not that Sarah's not feminine or anything, but, do you ever feel that Raela is just in need of your protection? Like, she's beautiful, and she's someone who would need you."

"Um, well—."

"And she's fun and funny. Like, um, she's just so much fun to be around. Not that Sarah isn't fun to be around, and, I mean, she's normally very fun and—I mean this stuff is so serious," and James cut himself off awkwardly.

There was a moment of uncomfortable silence. "Yea, they're both great," Anders finally said.

"So, I kind of want to eat in one of those restaurants we saw on that tour," James began abruptly.

"Yea, I thought the outdoor one looked neat," Anders agreed.

"Really? I was thinking more about the one with the columns."

And with the conversation clearly not about to return to me or Raela, I quietly pulled the door shut once more and climbed into bed.

Part of me was insulted at James's observations and beliefs about me. It was not my fault that I was born into such complications, though reason told me that it was not me or my life that he found off-putting. He had simply found a more intense interest elsewhere.

As I began to fall asleep, Anders' unusual comment about James being especially afraid that Raela would find out about our kiss came back to me. If he were developing feelings for her, even then, no wonder he wouldn't want word of our kiss to become common knowledge within our group.

Raela flipped sides in her sleep and I smiled a little to myself, happily finding that I wasn't jealous at all.

Chapter Eleven

Anders and James were the last ones downstairs to the kitchen the next morning, though when James did come down, he seemed energetic and well-rested. Anders entered the room just as Sylvia was spooning a grainy, beige oatmeal into our bowls. His black hair was stuck sloppily to one side, and I let out a half-stifled laugh. "Nice hair," I teased.

He immediately reached up and felt the top of his head, making a slight embarrassed face as he did so. Taking a seat at the table, though, he smoothly joked back, "Thanks, I've been working on it all night."

Everyone laughed and began making their own comments about the hours they had spent working on their own bedhead looks. My personal thoughts wandered to the night before and I wondered if Anders had been able to hear me or any thoughts I had had while listening in on him and James. Honestly, I wouldn't have classified any of my thoughts as fearful necessarily, and Anders gave me no look or signal that proved otherwise.

All of a sudden, I was brought out of my wonderings as a hot piece of oatmeal fell onto my lap from Sylvia's serving spoon.

"Ouch!" I yelled, pushing the chair back and jumping up, holding the hot portion on the skirt of my dress out and away from my body.

"I am so sorry," Sylvia said as she slammed down the bowl and began wiping at the spot with my napkin.

"It's all right. It's all right," I said, the feeling more shocking than painful and my discomfort only increasing as Sylvia awkwardly wiped my dress off at the front of my thighs. "Really," I said, managing to politely take my napkin from her so that I could wipe off the remaining oatmeal myself. "My dress is filthy anyway from traveling."

"All right," Sylvia hesitantly said, and she picked up the heavy oatmeal bowl and slowly began serving us once more. As she moved on to Raela's bowl next to mine, Sylvia said, "It's just—I suppose I'm a bit distracted today. I feel absolutely terrible about last night."

"What?" I said, and everyone looked at her, waiting for her to continue.

"For...you know. Talking ill about the scandal of Meraldia."

"Meraldia?" Raela asked.

"The woman in the jail?" Darius chimed in. "Why?"

Sylvia's face bore an instant look of alarm, her pale skin turning pasty like the walls around us.

I didn't know what to say, as I was utterly confused, when Anders thankfully spoke. "It's all right, Sylvia. We weren't offended even though Meraldia is Sarah's great-great-grandmother."

Sylvia let out her breath as her face instantly filled with rosy color. "Oh good, you did know. At first I was worried that I had spoken rashly and in ill manners about your great-great-grandmother," she said directly to me. "And then, just now, I was worried that maybe you didn't know you were related after all and so I was making a social mistake yet again!"

"No, no. It's fine," I said, my mouth dry. "We knew and we weren't offended. We were simply curious since she is a relative of mine, and we didn't want you to feel uncomfortable by talking about the connection," I said, and I immediately stuffed burning oatmeal into my mouth to discourage further conversation on the matter.

"Oh, good," Sylvia said, and she finished scooping the oatmeal into Raela's bowl. As Sylvia returned to the stove to tidy up, I spared a quick glance around the table. James, Raela, and Darius were all staring intently at their oatmeal while their minds were most assuredly elsewhere. Anders, on the other hand, was using his peripheral vision to look at me from across the table. I gave him a discreet nod of thanks and he nodded back. I burned my tongue twice on the oatmeal as I ate, anxious to finish it and go upstairs where we could talk out of earshot of Sylvia. Thankfully, the others seemed equally anxious because we all finished at roughly the same time.

"Thank you, Sylvia," I said overly cheery. "Breakfast was delicious."

"Oh, you're welcome," Sylvia replied, most of her natural hospitality evidently returned.

Our footsteps didn't thud heavily up the stairs as they had the night before, almost as if we were sneaking away from the kitchen. Indeed, that's how I knew I felt, and I was not completely certain that that's not what we were doing; I wondered if in addition to her hospitality, Sylvia was instructed to keep an eye on us and alert the Hersote rulers of any strange behavior or questions on our part. I hoped I was simply being paranoid, though the revelation of this strange family heritage and the fact that Octavia had obviously tried to hide the jail's true purpose during our tour made me uneasy.

As we came out onto the third floor common space, I looked at James who was following up the rear. "Can you stay by the stairs and listen for movement?" I whispered.

He nodded and immediately positioned himself at the top of the stairwell.

"Okay," Darius spoke first, his deep voice clear even at a whisper. "What's going on and how did you know that?" he asked Anders.

"My own type of magic," Anders said, "but could we discuss that part later? Right now I'm more interested in this family connection and what it could mean for us being here."

"So Meraldia is my great-great-grandmother and one of the Twelve," I said, working through things aloud. "She made a loophole of sorts in the spell so that she could destroy the immortality of the Hersotes. They didn't want me to know where she was, so I'm guessing they're just concerned that I'm here to free her and kill everyone and that's why we were treated like we were extremely dangerous at first?" It came out more as a question than a statement.

"I suppose, but why bring you here then?" James whispered from the stairs.

"He's right," Anders agreed. "It was clear from the beginning that they were afraid of you intending them harm," he said, giving me the smallest of nods to let me know that this was the fear he had heard thus far. "But specifically, if they're afraid of you coming to free your great-great-grandmother, why would they voluntarily bring you closer to her?"

"Also, let's not forget the meeting that they held last night," Raela said. "I'm assuming that's where Sylvia found out about your family. So they've obviously discussed it as a group so that they're all on the same page."

"Right," I said, considering the implications. "So, they brought me here knowing who I am. They seemed afraid at first, though then relieved."

"That change came after you explained that you don't know how to use magic," Darius reminded us.

"Right. So clearly, at least in their minds, I have the potential to be a threat."

"So they brought you here to keep an eye on you? And maybe keep you away from Merendinappa Island?" James offered.

"Probably," Raela agreed.

"Still, what kind of danger am I?" I asked. "I know I apparently wielded some form of magic accidentally in the past, but I'm not the one who enacted that spell, so I can't imagine I could use it to its full extent, even accidentally. Right?"

"Well, there is one person who would know the answer to that question," James said.

"Who?" I asked, not grasping his meaning. "We very well can't ask Meraldia," I said, wondering if she was to whom he was referring.

He shrugged his shoulders. "We could at least try."

"But what if we get caught and then they come to the conclusion that we really are trying to free Meraldia and kill everyone?" Darius asked. "I don't particularly want to be on these people's bad side."

"We may already be on their bad side. Plus, maybe she can give you some more answers—honest answers—about the blood moon," James said. "Clearly the rest of these people are going to be keeping secrets from us."

"I'm in," Raela said, smiling excitedly at James.

"Well, I agree it sounds good, though we don't know what kind of magic we're up against. It may very well keep us out entirely," Darius said.

"I have an idea that should allow us to play it off if we have to stop because the magic won't let us enter," Anders said, staring absently at the decorative table in thought. "How about we all go for a late dinner at one of those restaurants tonight?" he said, breaking his focus on the furniture and making quick eye contact with each of us.

"Sounds good to me," I said, smiling, excited to again be planning a course of action.

"Oo, the one with columns?" James asked.

Chapter Twelve

"I'm surprised there aren't more people in the streets still," James said quietly while staring out a window into the night. We were all seated around a circular table on the second floor of Gregoria's, the pillar theme continuing inside of the building where four thick pillars rose through the floor, the center of invisible, equal quadrants of the room.

"Yea, it's almost creepy how there seem to be no wanderers. Especially considering how much time these people have on their hands," Raela said.

"I guess it's made them actually slower and more patient. Like they're not going to wander aimlessly to pass time. Instead they're going to spend a week straight doing something indoors that we would maybe have spent an hour on," I guessed. My mother had lived like a regular mortal person, and I had always assumed that this was normal, though I now wondered if it was aided by the fact that she was in a mortal marriage.

Although we were still in the same clothes we had started our journey in, we had washed and dried them that morning, and had then taken turns bathing on the roof. It was amazing what a simple bath had done to my spirits. I no longer felt grimy, and I actually found myself feeling more awake and alert without a gross layer of oil on my skin, building around my nose. My dress was a noticeably lighter shade of brown once more, minus the sticky oatmeal smear from that morning and all of the dirt associated with our travels, and I actually felt rather well-off sitting in Gregoria's that night. Half of the approximately twenty tables were filled with people who shot us appraising looks occasionally, but much more discreetly than the looks given us the day of our arrival.

We took our time eating and then ordering dessert with the money given us by the Twelve through Sylvia once we had stated our intention to eat at Gregoria's that night.

"Mm. This chocolate pudding is to die for," Raela said, licking her spoon a bit overzealously for our subdued surroundings. "Agatha is going to regret not being here to try this."

Darius grunted in agreement, his mouth full of a syrupy piece of tangerine pie.

By the time we paid for our meal, all but one of the other tables was empty, and the traffic volume in the street below seemed to match as we saw one lone couple passing the restaurant below.

"Looks like a nice night to walk back to the house," Anders observed.

"Yea," James agreed, "though I think I want to take a little walk along the docks first. Anyway want to join me?" To the side I noticed a worker from the restaurant not far away, probably not listening, but possibly within earshot. Anders and James were obviously being very cautious.

"I'll go with you, James," Raela offered, as expected.

"Okay then. We'll see you two back at the house," I said, and we all walked downstairs together before James and Raela very naturally walked off in the opposite direction. Darius, Anders, and I walked at a leisurely pace toward the end of the street where the prison stood, faintly glowing and imposing. Passing by very close to it, and after a quick glance around to be sure no one was watching, we casually ducked into the shadowed space between the prison and the darkened building next to it.

We knew James and Raela weren't going to walk all the way to the docks before turning back and attempting to enter the prison's front doors, and so we weren't surprised when we heard voices coming from the direction of the prison's entrance not even ten minutes later. "The muggers went this way. Please hurry," Raela was saying.

Pressing up against the shadows of the adjacent building, we saw Raela and one young man hurry away, a second young man and James just behind them. As they ran past, James gave a casual cough, as if out of breath. A cough from James was a good sign; it meant that as far as they could tell, it was safe for us to enter. A clumsy trip from James would have been the signal to call off our planned infiltration.

I glanced at Anders in the darkness and he gave me a little nod; although not part of the official plan, I knew that Anders would be listening to the fears and worries of those around him to be sure that no one was concerned about an impending break-in in the immediate vicinity.

"Hurry," Darius said, and he shot out of the shadows first, hugging the front of the glowing prison as we speed-stepped to the entrance and slipped inside the front doors.

The inside looked more like a dank dungeon than the outside of the bright white building would suggest. We stood in a small corridor with crude, gray stone walls and a wooden plank floorboard that sloped steeply downward. Two torches stood on either side of the front door. Anders quickly reached for one and led the way downward, the temperature dropping as we went lower into the earth. At the bottom of the path, two level walkways split to the left and right. I guessed that we were about as deep in the earth as the structure above was tall, and I briefly wondered if the entire building were a shell or if an above-ground section were accessible elsewhere. Here, at the end of the slope, another torch brightly lit a small, but high-quality desk of finished marble. Two chairs sat on either side, pushed out away from the table where the guards must have been seated when Anders and Raela presumably entered with their pleas for help.

The path to the right was pitch black while the path to the left had a light at the end of the corridor, so it was an easy choice of which path to choose. We ran down the left and soon stood in front of a large open area dug out of the wall, lit with many candles and extremely out of place. This unusual cell—and I only thought of it as a cell for there was no other word in existence for what I was seeing—was probably almost the same size as my entire house. However there were no walls or partitions, no privacy. The walls and floor and ceiling were covered in that same bright white stone abundant in the city. A tub and toilet stood in the back far left corner while a red wood bed with bright yellow satin sheets stood in front of that. In the middle, there were a couple of trunks and many painted canvases, some half-finished on easels while other framed portraits lined the walls, most of them drawings of people. A circular bookshelf that rose to the ceiling was next to that, and then to the back right was an entire kitchen area with a large white stone table in front, close to the edge of the cell. And seated at this table was a beautiful woman, appearing perhaps thirty years of age, with incredibly light blonde hair and skin so pale it seemed to glow in the candlelight. Her fingers were long and thin, matching her over-thin body and the angular lines in her cheekbones and jaw. Her intense blue eyes were looking at us with extreme focus while her mouth half-smiled, almost playfully.

"I thought I'd see you soon," she said, and though she bore a strong resemblance to my mother, her voice was sharp and nasally in contrast to my mother's soft-spoken, gentle tones.

"How did you know?"

"No time. They'll be back soon. I answered everything for you in here," she said, and she stood, gracefully but quickly, and seemed to glide over the stone floor, her long pale green satin dress obscuring any view of her legs or feet. She reached directly for a book and then from behind it she withdrew a necklace with a purple stone dangling from it.

"Go somewhere away from the city when the moon is out. Don't let the moon's light touch it until you are away from where it might be overheard," she said.

I reached out my hand for it when the realization hit me—there were no bars to her jail cell. I instinctively took a step forward when Meraldia sternly ordered, "Stop right there. There might not be bars, but if you touch the invisible barrier, you'll be pulled in here, and neither of us will be able to pass it to get out. But," she continued, calmer as I had stopped, "I can pass inanimate objects through safely, which is how they collect things from me that must be taken out of here." She tossed me the necklace and I caught it. I then immediately handed it over to Anders who placed it deep in his pocket, clamping the pocket opening tight with his free hand.

"Thank you," I said, Darius on my right and Anders still holding the torch high on my left.

"Don't thank me. Thank you. I hope you can succeed in killing these miserable bastards," she said and I shuddered as she sneered, thankfully losing her physical likeness to my mother with this grotesque face.

Without further prompting, I ran off, back in the direction of the guard table, Anders at my side and Darius falling in behind us. Making a right turn, we hurried up the sharp slope, stopping at the front entrance only long enough to replace the torch and open the door a crack to look for people before stepping outside and shutting the doors behind us. The street was still empty, and we briskly walked in the direction of the house in which we were staying.

Turning onto the next street, we saw the two young men we had spotted following Raela and James just a bit ago. They said hello in passing and continued at a speed-walk back in the direction of the prison.

Turning onto yet another street, we saw James and Raela with four Hersotes around them, speaking in hushed tones.

"There you are!" I said, jogging over to them with Darius and Anders, and feeling the eyes of the Hersotes on me. "Are you two all right? We changed our minds and decided to take a walk with you, but we couldn't find you."

Raela was shaking visibly, her bun wobbling unsteadily on the top of her head, and James's lips had almost disappeared with how tight he was pressing them together.

"What happened?" Anders asked, seeming genuinely concerned.

"We were mugged," Raela said, apparently on the brink of tears.

"Mugged? You didn't have anything to steal," Darius said, his voice rising and falling in expressed confusion.

"Well, we know that, but whoever attacked us didn't," James said through gritted teeth before wrapping an arm around trembling Raela.

"So what happened exactly?" I asked.

"We were just telling these people," James said. "We were walking toward the docks when all of a sudden this guy jumped out of an alley. He threw us both to the ground and grabbed at our pockets. Raela gave him a swift kick and he ran off this way. We actually ran after him, but went for help at the nearest building after we lost sight of him."

"I'm still convinced that he wasn't trying to mug us. I think he was just doing it because we are mortals," Raela said, a minor look of accusation at the Hersotes around them.

"We will certainly look into the matter," one of the two male Hersotes said. "For now, perhaps you had better go back to the house where you're staying, just in case the man did mean you harm."

"All right," Raela eagerly agreed.

"We're here with you too now. Safety in numbers," Darius said, and we all thankfully made our way from the Hersotes, still in character for our ruse.

At the house, we went through the brief account once more for Sylvia's sake, who expressed excited concern before assuring us that it must have been a misunderstanding because no Hersote would purposefully hurt us.

We then bade her goodnight and went up to the third floor. It was only there that I noticed that Anders will still keeping the pocket of his pants held tight.

"Did you talk to her?" Raela whispered, falling backward onto the sofa, her black dress tightening around her belly as she did so, obviously still full following such a large supper.

"Yes. She gave us some necklace that she said would explain everything to us when held in moonlight."

"Then let's do it," James said, scanning my body with wide eyes.

"It's in Anders' pocket," I said in answer to his probing eyes. "But she warned us not to do it while people are around. She said to do it out of the city."

"Well let's go then," James insisted.

"Too risky," Darius said, sinking down on the sofa next to Raela. "We attracted enough attention for one night. Maybe tomorrow. And not all of us. Just let Anders and Sarah go. They're the two Hersotes."

"Oh come on," James said.

"No, he's right," Raela said, indicating Darius, and James gave a disappointed nod of assent.

"How are you going to take it out of your pocket?" I asked Anders who was covering a yawn with his free hand.

"Oh, I'm not taking it out," he answered. I plan on going right to bed like this and sleeping with a ridiculous number of blankets to keep any moonlight out. And then once the sun is up I won't have to worry about holding it there. And I don't plan on leaving the house at all tomorrow, and then tomorrow night we can go find out about it."

"Wow. That's kind of an intensely cautious plan," I said, the corner of my mouth turning up in a smile nonetheless.

"I'm not taking any chances with this," he said, returning the slight smile.

"Well, in that case," Darius said, slapping his knees in determination, "I'm going to bed."

"Sounds like a good idea," Raela said, and she immediately stood. "Good night guys," she said as she walked into our bedroom. I gave the boys a little wave before following her.

Our bedroom was covered in the moon's light, having opened the curtains earlier that day. Raela sighed and simply sank onto her bed at the opposite end of the room.

"How are you doing, Raela?" I asked as I shut the curtains.

Her voice came quietly out of the darkness. "All right," she said. "I miss Celia. But I'm doing all right."

"I'm glad," I said quietly as I took off my brown shoes, stretching my toes in the cool night air.

"I do miss my other family members too, though. And Agatha, and even Gregory, I guess," she said a minute later, after I had curled up on my bed. "I'm glad I'm here, though. With all of you, I mean."

"I'm glad you are too," I said, and I closed my eyes, wondering how Agatha and Gregory were making out in Harpson and also thinking of my dad, hoping he wasn't sick with worry, staring out at the empty village road through his half-moon glasses, waiting for me to come home.

Chapter Thirteen

"It's weird with it just the two of us," I said quietly, only realizing how awkward the sentence sounded after the words had fled my mouth. "I mean, not because of you. Because we've been in a group this whole time, so it feels weird separating for a bit," I rambled, reminding myself of James.

Anders let out a single-breath laugh. "Don't worry. I knew what you were saying."

We passed by the two Grotanian restaurants known to us, fairly quiet, but not deserted at this semi-late hour.

"Still," Anders continued in a hushed tone, "I think it's safer if we don't all travel out of the city in a conspicuous group."

"Oh, I agree," I said, and we were silent as we walked calmly in the direction of the boats and docks before making a left, along the rocky shoreline. The waves crashed against the rocks, and the moon created a long beam of light along the tranquil sea beyond, making a path toward home.

"In here," Anders said suddenly, looking around to be sure we weren't being followed. The trees grew thick to our left, and as we entered their tangled mass, each of us tripped a few times, climbing upward with the intense slope of the land in that area.

"I hope we'll be able to see the moon once we decide we're far enough away from the city," I said, surveying the thick trees around us and the darkness enveloping us.

"There's got to be some area that's cleared enough," Anders said.

A few more minutes passed. "So, have you decided when, or even if for that matter, you're going to tell our friends that you're a Slyton and not a Hersote?"

"I'll tell them," Anders answered, stepping over a fallen log, distinctly dark on the shadowed ground. "The time just hasn't felt right yet."

I nodded in the darkness. "Speaking of being a Slyton," I continued hesitantly, "I've noticed the moon is close to full."

"Yea," he said uneasily.

"What should we do? I'm guessing you've only got a few more days."

He sighed deeply, and I heard a bush shake as his clothes must have become briefly caught on it. "I'm not exactly sure. I suppose I'll have to explain my situation to the others before then, and then maybe you could lock me in your bedroom for the night since that's the only room with an actual door."

"I don't think the windows lock. Plus, the door locks from the inside."

"Hm. Maybe Darius could figure something out then. Like chains or something."

"Why do you need to lock yourself up anyway? I mean, I know you become mean or something, but what exactly happens?"

"It's not that we just become generically mean. We become the worst versions of ourselves. So any negative thoughts, fears, and emotions I have—they all come to the surface. So if I'm feeling angry and wishing I could punch something, I would probably give in to that. Or if there's some subconscious part of me that's jealous, I would just take action to solve the situation in which I find myself jealous. So your father would lock us in our house to prevent us from damaging things or other people—physically, yes, but even just emotionally."

"Did he lock you all together?"

"No. We didn't want to hurt each other either. We all had our own rooms that locked from the outside. That helped, but it still didn't always make it easy. I can remember one time my mother and father were screaming at each other from their own rooms. The next morning, your father said he couldn't hear much from your house, so that was a relief. And then there's the doors," he said with a swallow. "Locking us in our rooms helps prevent us from searching them out."

I knew immediately that he was not referring to the normal doors found in his house. "Do you want to enter a door to hell on the full moon nights?" I asked, hoping that any subconscious judgment was not present in my tone of voice.

He took a deep breath. "Yes," he said finally, and I looked for his eyes in the darkness, the whites around his dark irises shining back at me. "Please don't be frightened of me," he said, almost timidly.

"I'm sorry," I stuttered. "I was just surprised, is all. I just never pictured you wanting to go to hell at any point in time."

"It's powerful, the pull on those nights. I…. Well, I think I would be able to ignore my more sinful urges if not locked up, but it would be very difficult. I just—I just wish I weren't a Slyton. It's difficult to be one."

"Were Slytons made in hell?" I asked, not knowing anything about their supposed origins.

"It's been thousands of years supposedly, and Slytons have lost track of the truth in that time, I'm sure." I could hear the ironic laugh in his voice as he spoke next. "Slytons aren't exactly known for the truth anyway since we thrive on fear and deception. Anyway, legend holds that the first Slyton was actually a king. I don't know from which kingdom, but I believe the name Slyton is derived from the king's name. Anyway, his kingdom was being attacked by an outside invader. And somehow he made a deal with the devil. He said he needed a way to hear the fears of his enemies so that he could exploit them. And so that's what he was given. It's a weird feeling, though, that horrible knowledge, and so after he won the war, the king still used his newfound power to manipulate those around him. During the next several years, he developed some sort of bond with the devil, meeting him at night. Legend then holds that the king himself grew so dark and evil that he asked for a way to commune with the devil more permanently. And so the devil created a door to hell for the king, which showed itself on the night of the full moon—the night when there is the most light from which to escape to the darkness."

I tripped, but quietly, and quickly stood up and continued our ascent, not wishing to break the flow of Anders' story.

"The devil made the king immortal at this point, as entering hell necessitated that since it is not a location for mortals. And apparently the king stayed there for a time, perhaps a century or more. But then the devil instructed him to go back through a door because he had found a woman as twisted as the king. The king and woman—I believe legend holds her as a peasant woman—married, or some dark equivalent I suppose. And they had five kids together, each of them an immortal Slyton as well. With the devil's "adopted offspring," as we often refer to them, multiplying, the devil created more doors, appearing around the world as more and more Slytons were born. And so Slytons can come and go from this horrible home as they please, though the urge to stay in hell is much stronger than the urge to leave and, I guess it's hoped, wreak havoc on this world."

"How many Slytons are there?" I asked.

"I have no idea. I don't think there are many in our world, though. I remember my mother and father once guessing a couple hundred, though there are probably thousands that remain in hell."

The slope of the land started to become more even and the trees began to thin.

"So how did any of you become good?"

He laughed again, without humor this time. "Thanks for calling me 'good.'"

"I'm serious," I said. "You're obviously good. It's not your fault you were born a Slyton. You're kind and caring, and you wanted to explore the blood moon at Merendinappa because you didn't want to hurt anyone."

"Well, thank you," he said seriously.

"But for real, how did that happen for some of you?"

"We may have been cursed by this awful, ancient deal with the devil, but we were still made by God. While predisposed to something more sinister, we still have free will."

And a moon beam broke upon us.

"The trees are definitely thinning," Anders said excitedly, and he picked up the pace.

Only a few more minutes of speed walking and we came to a tiny clearing, the moon clearly visible high above us. The location did something to remind me of the clearing among the trees on Merendinappa, and I shivered, half-expecting the moon to change to blood, even though the predicted blood moon was still a couple of months away.

Without a word, Anders reached into his pants pocket and withdrew a knife. He then pulled up the bottom of one of his pant legs, cutting at it with the knife. I had sewn the stone into the bottom of his black pants that day, safe from the moon's rays while walking this night.

With one forceful swipe, the purple stone and brilliant gold chain fell from their secret pocket, landing with a soft thud on the grassy ground. It started glowing immediately, its purple becoming a pulsating aura around it, like a fire.

"Hello blood of my blood," the cutting voice spoke, sounding like a mischievous specter in the moonlight. "I'm so glad you've found me in time for the coming blood moon. So I'm guessing you have some questions.

One of the Twelve, Geraldine, still visits me occasionally, and she told me that you were in the city, wondering what type of weird power you have through the blood moon. I'm glad you came to retrieve this amulet I made. Anyway, as I hope you're well aware, immortality is a curse, a horrible mistake, not a blessing. It makes us obsolete, tortured here for eternity. It allows our ambitions to run wild and unchecked, when time is not an issue. The other Hersotes are planning something, but Geraldine wasn't able to hint at what—I'm afraid to find out. I'm hoping that you can kill us all before they embrace their evil even more fully."

I glanced at Anders, his dark eyebrows drawn down in concentration.

"Anyway, I was found by a growing group of Hersotes when I lived in Meldionia a long time ago. I'm extremely gifted in promoting and manipulating rhythms, and so I had gained some level of fame in helping people through various health problems—a heart attack, a troubled child labor, those sorts of things. Well, the Hersotes explained their plan to combine their various talents to create immortality, pointing out how useful and necessary rhythm was, to keep a heart beating forever, a lung continuously taking in breath. And so I agreed. After all, I was honored to be chosen and excited about the prospect of cheating death permanently! But as the time approached, I began to grow nervous. After all, forever is a long time to live on this planet. And the relayed ambitions of some of the other Hersotes were a bit concerning. So, I began to plan my portion, but also an escape route of sorts. We were going to direct our spell into the blood moon, and the moon just so happens to be my throsote too. So, the night we enacted our little spell, covering all Hersotes on the planet with the curse of immortality, I silently included a little caveat—that I would be able to pull from the power of our combined spell while manipulating my key ingredient on the night of a blood moon, instantly stopping the rhythm that immortals depend on.

"Setting up our Hersote kingdom at Merendinappa, I barely experienced my immortality in the outside world before I saw what a huge mistake it was indeed. The first few decades, I watched the non-Hersote spouses who came over with their grooms and brides age and begin their slow decay. I went to the other Twelve about this problem, and they explained, as I sadly already suspected they would say, that our spell of immortality could not be granted to everybody. There was this sort of superiority present in their determination, and I just knew that they wanted the non-Hersotes to die—

that they weren't worthy of immortality.

"And so I realized that I would need to call on my way out and die eventually, at the next blood moon, more than two thousand years away. However, in the meantime, my questions and expressed doubts about our immortality began to worry the other Twelve. Geraldine began to warn me periodically about how much I was saying, and I tried to watch my tongue, but my words still leaked out. And so I worried that two thousand years was a bit far away to ensure that I would be free and able to enact my reverse-spell. And so forty years after the curse, I sat down and wrote a letter to my son.

"At this point I should explain that right before I was originally approached by the other Hersotes, I had given birth to a son. I was not married to his father, but still lived with him at the time. And while I had no desire to actually marry that man, I was growing weary of the disapproving looks of people in the market. And so it was actually a bit of a relief when I was met by the Hersotes, looking only at my incredible powers with awe instead of my tired face with judgment. And so I simply up and left my two-month-old son with his father and never looked back until it came time for me to write that letter. A Hersote I had met cast a detection spell on it, increasing its chances of finding my son, wherever he was, if he were even still alive. Only a few days after I sent off this letter, the other Twelve arrested me. They questioned me about my misgivings, and through a truth-magic forced a confession about my escape plan. And so they threw me in a prison where I had no access to the moon's rays so that I could not call down my reverse-spell. But," and I could hear the calculating smile in her pause, "they didn't know about the letter I had sent to my son.

"In the letter, I explained the Hersotes' only other hope for death if I was incarcerated, as I feared. I explained that a Hersote of my blood—a direct descendent—could also call the spell down from the blood moon. As I left when my son was so young, and never heard of him voyage to Merendinappa Island, I guessed he had taken after his non-magical Jersos father. I told him if this was the case, he needed to find a Hersote and father a magical, and possibly immortal, child. In this way, my blood, and thus his blood, would be passed down to stop the evil Hersotes. I played up the intentions of the Hersotes in the letter, but I wanted him to take this task seriously. Years passed, I suppose, though it's difficult to track time in my own underground world. But then one day Geraldine paid me a visit, exclaiming that she had had no idea I had once given birth to a son. He had married some poor Hersote girl and together they had had a daughter before her mother discovered my son's heritage and intentions and killed him. I'm very lucky," she continued without a pause after relaying the death of her only child, "that he managed to father a child before he was discovered and killed. After all, as I'm sure you're aware, it is not common for a woman Hersote to have a child, as the rhythm and timing of our bodies was greatly affected through immortality."

"Doesn't she care about her son?" Anders whispered lightning-fast, and I looked up and saw his disgusted expression directed toward the glowing stone. As my thoughts were with his, I assumed my expression was similar.

"So, anyway, I never knew what happened with this daughter, if my son was able to explain her purpose or anything, and I was left never really knowing, only learning through Geraldine that eventually my granddaughter had given birth to another girl who left Grotania, where I had been moved when the Hersotes moved, desiring more room. I never heard anything more about the girl who left, and to be honest I'm not entirely sure that you are her or if you are a descendent of hers, since rumor has it that you killed your own immortal mother."

Anders looked at me questioningly. "My mother is the girl who left Grotania," I said, finding that my lineage was a lot to take in even for me.

"One fact remains," Meraldia's voice cut over mine. "You must be a descendent of mine because Geraldine managed to let me know that you were able to call down death at Merendinappa Island. That's wonderful news. It means that this time of waiting is almost over for me.

"So now for your instructions. All you have to do is make yourself present and bathed in the blood moon's rays. Then simply think of Hersotes in a very general fashion. The blood will spread around our planet. It will be much like that blood moon you saw at Merendinappa Island, except that it will be the real magic—capable of so much more than that meager shadow of magic you saw before. That being said, you are very lucky that your thoughts were with your mother at the time because otherwise I'd imagine death would have simply sought out the nearest Hersote—you."

I swallowed, guilt washing over me anew. Anders reached a hand over the glowing stone and held mine as we stood there, heads pointed down at the invisible voice.

"So it would seem that luck was on your side," Meraldia's nasal, insensitive voice continued. "The good news is you don't even have to focus on your own throsote since it's really just my magic working through you. So this will all be very simple, and hopefully in a couple more months, we'll all be dead."

And just like that, the stone stopped glowing.

"That—that's it?" Anders said, shocked, his voice sounding loud in the sudden darkness.

"I…guess so," I said, staring blankly at the jewel as it slowly came back into focus under the natural light of the moon.

"And what's a throsote?" Anders demanded of the stone.

"It's like a talisman of sorts. It's something that Hersotes channel their magic through. For Meraldia, I guess it was the moon. Throsotes can sometimes be passed down through generations, though sometimes a person discovers that they are completely different. I never bothered to ask my mother what hers was."

"Can you choose them?" Anders asked, and I looked away from the stone and into his eyes looking slightly down into mine.

"No. Hersotes must take time to discover theirs. I never took the time to discover mine. I wanted nothing to do with magic."

We were silent for a minute, each staring at the jeweled necklace on the ground, not daring to touch it.

"I don't like her," Anders finally said.

"Me neither."

"Basically the only thing I can agree with her on is that immortality seems to be a curse. Everything around us changes, but we're stuck here, watching others succumb to death, with no hope of following them into the afterlife. But…she said all of you would die. I—I don't want you to die in a couple of months."

I coughed on my dry throat. "I don't want to die either. Perhaps one day, but I'm only eighteen—a legitimate, real eighteen. So maybe I could simply stay out of the blood moon? Though what's this plan the Hersotes are up to?"

Anders nodded thoughtfully. "We could ask about it—innocently of course. Maybe they might give something away."

The word "away" had barely left Anders' lips when the unfortunately familiar frozen feeling from Merendinappa Island overwhelmed us both, our eyes swiveling in our still heads, and then locking on each other.

"I have them!" a voice called from behind me.

"What are they doing up here?" another voice demanded angrily.

Although I couldn't look at them, I could hear the movements of several bodies right behind me.

"Look!" a man's deep voice called, and his massive body appeared at our sides where he bent down and picked up the purple stone necklace.

He held it up high and then retraced his steps behind me where, after a few seconds, a squeaky female voice declared, "It's from Meraldia. I told you that we should be keeping a closer eye on them."

"That settles it," a familiar deep female voice—Octavia's—stated strongly. "To the Confinement. And for good measure, bring me their other friends as well."

Anders' frozen expression of thoughtfulness from before did not match the horror I assumed he was now feeling too.

Chapter Fourteen

Frozen in a standing position, one of the Hersotes used magic to float us just above the ground all the way back through the woods and to the city. The group that had been spying on us had us facing forward, away from them, and so I watched in desperate helplessness as we were sent away from the freedom of the woods and then the shoreline and beckoning ocean beyond. Then, entering the city, I was reminded that this still represented a freedom of sorts; after all, if we were taken to the Confinement, it was likely that we would never see the outdoors again. But with my neck frozen in place, I could not even take one good, final look at the stars, relying on my frenzied peripheral vision.

With the Confinement before us, I tried to inhale deeply, finding only an unsatisfactory, shallow scent of salt air reaching my nostrils before the doors were opened before us and then quickly closed.

The quiet Hersotes behind us, who had taken the torches from the wall to guide their steps, perked up a bit as our final destination grew closer.

"Should we place them in the same cell even though they're opposite genders?" a man's voice asked.

"This is why I said we should have built more than the two cells, just in case!" the squeaky female voice from before piped up.

"We'll just have to place them together for now," Octavia responded. "It's not ideal, I agree, though I'm not taking the chance of placing her with Meraldia."

And so at the bottom of the pathway, attracting the excited attention of the two guards on duty, I was not surprised when our group made a right, down the dark hall opposite Meraldia's.

A mirror only in the layout of the cell in relation to the hallway, I was taken aback to see that the interior of the cell was nothing like Meraldia's unusually comfortable interior. The stone walls in this cut-out rectangle matched the roughly chiseled gray of the walls in the hall, as did the simple wooden floorboards throughout. For furniture, there stood only a single bed covered in a thick layer of dust, and a tub and toilet in the left back corner.

We were held still only for a second before a great push, like a strong windstorm, catapulted us forward into this cell. The feeling took my breath away for a moment, and it took a bit of gasping for air for me to realize that my body was no longer frozen in place and I was instead kneeling awkwardly on the floorboards. Raising my head, I found that I was looking at the back wall, but quickly looked for Anders, who I thankfully found right next to me, his eyes already looking back into mine. In unison then, we turned to look outward at our captors. It was odd; it appeared like we could simply leave the cell at any time without bars present, a cruel illusion of freedom.

"Go ahead," Octavia said with a malicious smile, her green eyes almost neon in the light of the torches and her golden hair almost as reflective. "Touch the barrier. I know you want to."

I looked at Anders for help, who simply stood without energy or enthusiasm and walked forward, his arms outstretched before him. Where I would have expected it, he came to a spot, his hands pressed flat against the air as if there were a wall there.

"Nice, isn't it?" Octavia said. "It will allow us to bring you your food and perhaps additional belongings for your cell as time passes. But it will not allow you out. Also, if anyone were to ever have a rescue mission in mind, it will pull anyone who touches the barrier from this side in with you, so unless you're feeling absolutely wicked, I wouldn't let anyone try." She tucked her hair behind both ears slowly before continuing. "As far as your furnishings go, I expect you've seen Meraldia's cell. Behave yourself and we'll permit you small luxuries, though apparently Meraldia needs to have hers removed after her little smuggling act with that stone. We will find you a second bed as soon as possible, though—we have standards and morals."

I snorted, turning my head toward the dusty bed and wondering if the sheets were really a charcoal gray if cleaned.

"All right, well, good night, and welcome home," Octavia ended simply and she nodded toward the wall where one of the Hersotes with a torch placed the fire, leaving us a single light out of our reach. Octavia then spun on her heels and marched off, the six other Hersotes in her company giddy in their animated departure, though silent with their tongues.

Left alone in the shadows, we each stood silent and motionless for several minutes. Finally, Anders spoke. "This is it then," he said, and his voice came out in more of a monotone shock than trembling fear.

"Yes," I said, the single syllable catching and wavering in my own throat.

He walked over to the bed and I followed, watching as he put a hand on it and drew it back up, leaving a clear handprint on the dusty fabric. He reached forward then and began to brush it off, though burst into a coughing fit only a second later.

"Here, I'll take care of it," I said, reaching forward and gathering up the sheet into a ball of sorts in an attempt to contain the dust for the moment.

"Sorry," Anders said, the coughing beginning to subside as I reached the empty, back right corner.

"It's all right," I said, letting the sheet drop and instantly enveloping myself in a cloud of dust. "I'll just shake it out good over here."

I did so, finding that the dust did not remain in the corner as I had fruitlessly hoped. Returning to Anders with the beaten and noticeably cleaner sheet, I saw that he was wiping away the accumulated dust on the actual bedframe, rubbing at his eyes fiercely with his free hand.

"Dust allergy?" I asked.

"Apparently," he said, sniffing.

"Well, we don't have to go to sleep right this second, I said, and looking around the empty cell, I walked to the far left wall and simply took a seat against the cool stone and rough floorboards.

Anders followed my lead and sat down next to me. In what had become somewhat familiar over the last couple of weeks, I reached out my hand and grabbed hold of his. He squeezed mine reassuringly in response before actually pulling his hand from mine and instead wrapping his entire arm around my shoulders, pulling me close. Something about this comforting contact caused my emotions to break, and I burst into long, quiet sobs, my head against his shoulder as Anders silently shook next to me.

Chapter Fifteen

"Are you two sleeping?" a chipper female voice asked.

My head snapped upward at once, and I felt Anders jerk next to me, his arm dropping from around me in startled surprise.

At the barrier of our cell stood an apparently young woman, backlit mysteriously from the single torch on the far wall of the hallway.

"Sorry to wake you. Did you two sleep that way all night?" she asked.

"Um…if it's morning, I suppose we did," I said, though the lighting obviously appeared no different.

"Yes, it's late morning actually," she said. "Don't worry—I'm sure you'll get used to the light situation here," she reassured us pleasantly, as if she were telling us of a simple change, like she were offering us strawberry jam over customary grape.

"Anyway," she continued, "my name is Urga. I'm one of the Twelve. I've brought you two a few belongings to help keep you more comfortable for now." And with that, she used an unseen force to float items from just out of sight in the hallway into view, the largest of which was a bedframe, already made up with burgundy sheets.

"Stand back," she said, and she used her magic to glide the large piece of furniture into our cell, followed by two hefty boxes. "One of those boxes contains an assortment of candles and fire starters. The other contains dry goods. Eventually we can send in some parts for you to assemble a kitchen," she said. "But for now you can just have the two beds and bathroom items in here, though that won't last for long, of course."

"Are you taking the other bed back?" I asked uncertainly while Anders opened one of the boxes.

"Well, when he dies soon," Urga said, and my heart sped up forcefully at her words before remembering that Anders couldn't die, a secret that I determined would be out soon enough as Anders did not age past his choosing.

Anders had paused in his opening of the box. "Are you going to kill me?" he asked, his words drawn out in incomprehension.

"Oh no. I mean when you die—probably of old age, of course, but in the blink of an eye for those of us with all the time in the world," Urga responded happily.

"Ah," he simply said, continuing to open the box before him. He pulled out a candle and fire stone and lit the first one, placing it on the floor.

"Just careful not to knock them over, of course," Urga said. "With the wooden floor you two have right now, you don't want to hasten your inevitable demise, and even though you can't die," she said, focusing on me, "burning in fire is still rather unpleasant I've heard."

I took the first candle as Anders continued lighting more and brought it close to the barrier, lighting the area in front of Urga. "Have any of you been burned?" I asked, studying this member of the Twelve carefully. She looked perhaps twenty-five, though if she were one of the Twelve she was obviously much older. With voluminous blonde hair wrapped around a baby face, she looked naturally friendly, though her words had been blunt and harsh wrapped in a disarming demeanor. Her unusually wide hips were visible beneath her tight green dress, and although thin, her body frame looked as if it longed to be fuller.

"Well, yes," Urga said in answer to my question. "Hersotes have been burned, cut, fallen from incomprehensible heights." I thought back to Anders and my own fall in front of our friends and shivered. "Have you never been about to die or be seriously injured?" She continued without waiting for an answer, "It doesn't really hurt. Some have described tingling or a dazed feeling. One girl I spoke to who was on fire for a time said that it tingled nonstop as her body was constantly healing and protecting itself from the flames. That sort of stuff is the work of Bethany, Ruth, Hallia, and Lydia."

"They're part of the Twelve too?" I asked, and Anders finally stopped lighting candles, our cell brightly lit behind us.

"Oh yes," she said. "Bethany is strong in protectant magic, which is why when you are injured or burned, it doesn't really do anything in the first place. Ruth is strong in regeneration, so although a knife could, say, enter you and not hurt you thanks to Bethany, your body fixes itself to appear just like it always did at lightning speed because of Ruth. And then Hallia can stave off death for just a short time, which is all that's needed to be helpful for Bethany and Ruth's part in the spell to take effect. So if, for example, your head were cut off, Hallia's magic can keep your body briefly alive as it heals itself almost instantly behind the blade. Of course, this magic works better with Ruth and Bethany's magic. After all, if your head were actually able to be fully severed from your body, being alive for a time after wouldn't prove very useful if you can't get it back on." Urga laughed slightly at the thought, as Anders drew up alongside of me, both of us a mere foot from Urga.

"And who was the fourth woman you named?"

"Oh, Lydia. She can block pain, which is important if you're going to be standing in the middle of a fire."

"What's your power, Urga, that made you one of the Twelve?" I asked, inexplicably eager to keep the conversation going with this unique visitor.

"Oh, mine isn't as important as most of the others', though still helpful. I have this strange power to combat gravity—not common in the slightest. It's useful medicinally for things like aching knees, slumping backs. You know, just things to help make our unlimited life here as pleasant as possible."

"What are the other Twelve's powers?" Anders asked.

"Well, Octavia has health, specifically when it comes to battling illnesses. Geraldine can slow down bodily functions, which is useful if you were ever without food for a long period of time. Meraldia does cycles, though I expect you already knew that. Daria has the hardest to describe—this sort of mind power. But it's what helps you control the point at which you stop aging. Amber has this sort of fail-safe magic we needed. It allows your body to recycle things like air and food indefinitely if you were unable to breathe or eat or something, though ideally Geraldine's magic would make this necessary in only extreme circumstances. Then Lily has the power of consciousness. After all, immortality would be pretty boring if we were stuck in comas. And then…I feel like I'm forgetting one person. Oh! Margaret, of course! She holds the magic of combination. She used it as a chef before she met us, if you can believe that! Using her magic of combination to make food that was delicious. I mean, don't get me wrong, that's useful. She runs Eliona's, but when we recruited her to become one of the Twelve, she was able to put her magic to such a higher use, combining all of our various talents before placing them into her throsote for safekeeping, which as you unfortunately seem aware, is the moon." It was the only sour hint in her voice during the conversation.

"Is it true that you never bothered searching out your own throsote and discovering your own type of magic?" she suddenly asked, her voice pleasantly calm yet her blue eyes wide with surprise.

"Yes," I simply said.

"Fascinating," she said.

"What happened to our friends?" I asked abruptly, the question having been gnawing at me throughout the night.

"Oh, I'm not sure," she said dismissively. "Well, I should be heading out. I have a lot I'd like to accomplish. It was nice talking to you, though!" and without a pause, she turned around and bounced with a lively step away from our cell.

"Hungry?" Anders asked simply once Urga was out of sight.

"Sure," I said, turning around and opening up the box of food, which consisted mostly of various crackers, jams, and juices.

"We both sat on top of the new, far cleaner bed, munching on the first container of crackers we came across.

I glanced around our dingy new home and shivered, despite the temperature being comfortable. I was terrified because this was not simply designed to be the rest of my life—this was designed to be my forever.

As another shiver went through me, I felt Anders' eyes resting on me. Upon making eye contact, he actually let out the hint of a smile. "So," he began, a bit of cracker still in his mouth, "what do you want to talk about?"

I burst into nervous laughter. We would be able to ask each other that question for all of eternity, though there was something oddly comical about his bald approach to our reality that somehow made me relax. At least we weren't alone.

Chapter Sixteen

"Wait, where's King Wheat?" I asked, looking around us at the floor.

"Oh, I ate him," Anders said deadpan, though as I looked at him, his deep brown eyes twinkled with laughter in the candlelight.

"You ate him? You're not supposed to do that!" I burst into giggles, and he joined in.

We were sitting on the floor in the middle of our cell, building an elaborate castle out of the myriad of crackers we had been given.

"No worries. I'll just build Queen Oat a new husband," Anders said, and he reached into what we had deemed our cracker box, our laughter still not quite suppressed.

"Laughter already on day three of your confinement? Determined to make the best of your time?" a husky female voice asked. Our laughter ceased immediately as we looked at the first visitor we had had since Urga. "What are you doing with your food? Didn't your mother ever teach you it isn't polite to play with your food, or did she die before she could teach you manners?"

Anders rose to his feet defensively and marched straight to the edge of our cell, his face only inches away from our new visitor's, her eyes only slightly lower than his. As he had approached, I thought I caught the woman flinch very slightly, though she covered up this minor mistake with her cool and controlled speech and perfectly straight posture.

"I wanted to come and see how you two were making out in your new forever home. And I wanted to get a glimpse myself of the girl who meant us all such harm when we had done nothing to her," she said, stepping to the side to see me around Anders.

"Well, here I am, though I did not intend you harm."

"Sure, sweetie," she said, her harsh voice coming out of what sounded like a constricted throat. She stared at me with an uncomfortable intensity.

"Have you just come to look at us?" Anders asked, stepping in front of her gaze yet again.

She finally looked at him once more. "I also brought some more food," she said, and she withdrew a small bundle from her dress pocket and tossed it through the barrier. Neither of us made a move toward it.

"It's some cheese," she said, so you might want to eat it sooner rather than later. "Especially while you're both still alive. You see," she said, drawing even closer to Anders, "it feels like a waste to feed you and harbor you when you were colluding with someone who was hoping to murder an entire group of people. So I'll be talking to the other Twelve—well, eleven technically," she corrected herself, sparing a malicious glance for me around Anders, "about just killing you now. I know you'll probably be dead in fifty years or so, but why wait? Though I've always been the impatient one of the group."

I stood. "Who are you?" I demanded, my fists clenched at my sides. I was furious at this woman's disregard for Anders' life, even though it was in no real danger.

"Margaret," she answered, her lips slightly upturned in disgust as she looked at me. "I'm one of the Twelve. An important one."

"Oh, yes," I said, remembering Urga's brief account of the Twelve and Margaret's place as the one with the magic of combination. "You own Eliona's. We thankfully chose to eat at Gregoria's not long ago."

She snickered at me. "I really don't need your business."

"But you need to mock and stare at us?" Anders said sternly.

"Very well, I'll leave you to your childish games. I just wanted to see you with my own eyes." And she was gone, leaving us angered and shaking.

We quietly stewed for a time, the extent of which had already grown difficult to gauge in our sun- and moonless prison.

"I believe," I eventually said, "that you were about to reconstruct King Wheat."

Anders turned and walked back over to me, the hint of a smile returning to his face. "You don't mind these childish games?"

"As long as you don't mind that I ate Queen Oat right before you turned around."

And we managed to push feelings from our brief meeting with Margaret aside as we continued our lighthearted, quite silly game.

What we assumed was that night, we both climbed into our beds, blowing out most of the candles first. We kept our beds only a few feet apart from each other even though the cell was quite large. It simply felt safer that way, having each other so near.

As soon as we were quiet and settled, my thoughts raged at me, though I tried to keep my anger and panic at bay—the sadness and hopelessness that playing silly games with crackers seemed to keep away. A tear rolled from my eye and back toward my temple, onto my stale pillow.

"Are you all right?" Anders' voice asked quietly.

"Yes," I said, reaching up and wiping at the wet stream on my face. I took a deep breath. "I'm so sorry, Anders."

"You didn't do anything."

"I feel like this is all my fault. I'm the one who told you about the blood moon."

"I wanted you to. I wanted to go with you."

"Still…," I trailed off. "I just—we'll never see our families again. I'll never see my father. And what about your little sister? They might not even find out what happened to us. And we still haven't heard about Raela or James or Darius. And we'll never see the sun, or the moon, or the stars, or feel the wind or listen to a bird singing."

Anders sighed from his bed. "It'll be all right."

"How can you say that?" I asked, turning my head in his direction. "What if we become like Meraldia over time? Maybe that's what being in this sort of eternal prison does to you—makes you cold and calculating, unnaturally patient bordering on insane."

His profile remained staring calmly at the ceiling. "We won't end up like Meraldia. She was cold and calculating even before she became immortal. Like how she left her baby so easily and then used him as a pawn later. As if she hadn't done enough damage to him by simply leaving him for what she thought was better."

I turned my face back toward the stone ceiling.

"Well, I do hope you're right and that we won't become like her. I am sorry, though," I insisted.

"There's no need to be sorry, I told you."

We were both quiet briefly before I spoke again. "I'm sorry that your dream to fight for love with some mortal woman is lost too." I remembered this unusual confession of his from the ship to Merendinappa and how I couldn't completely relate. Now, though, an adventure for love seemed painfully appealing, as we had discovered that we were unwittingly on an adventure for death.

Anders laughed ever so slightly next to me. "You know," he said, and I heard him shift. Turning toward him I saw that he had pushed himself up on one arm, staring at me in the darkness. "I might never find an adventurous mortal girl. But I can think of worse people to spend eternity with."

I smiled and let out a small laugh. "You're not so bad yourself," I said, and he settled back down into his bed with a satisfied grin on his pale face.

I hadn't thought I was tired, but I was shortly aware of being woken up.

I shot straight up in bed, startled by an unfamiliar female voice. Anders nearby did the same thing and the voice immediately responded to our motion. "I am so sorry," said a seemingly kind voice, cracked with age. "I didn't mean to wake you. I couldn't sleep, though, and figured that with the sun and moon hidden from you, you might very well be awake at this late hour."

I rubbed at one of my eyes, trying to force them to adjust against the sudden light. She had brought down a torch with her, which she was holding instead of placing in the wall holder.

"Who are you?" Anders asked, his voice groggy with sleep.

"My name is Geraldine. I'm one of the Twelve."

"You're—you're old!" I exclaimed, and Geraldine laughed raucously in response. Her face was lined with creases and her long, straight hair was completely silver. Her eyes, unlike most Hersotes', were dark, at least as they appeared in the shadows and torchlight.

"Well, not much older than the other Twelve, though they found me when I was a good forty or so years older than most of them. Our spell didn't reverse time. It only allowed us to stop it. But don't you worry about me—I still feel quite spritely for a woman of 2,132.

"So why are you here? Come to stare at us too?" Anders asked angrily.

She shook her head in response. "Oh, I heard that Margaret had been here to see you earlier today. She's a bit of an antagonist, no? Still, I came here suspecting that you might be too, what with you being Margaret's great-great-granddaughter," she said, staring directly at me.

"No, Meraldia is my great-great-grandmother," I said, confused.

"Oh, I know that, of course! I mean with Margaret being your other great-great-grandmother. You know, since it was her daughter who unwittingly married Meraldia's son. Of course it was Margaret who killed him when she found out what he was about."

I shook my head. "That awful woman is my great-great-grandmother?"

"I'm sorry to break that bad news to you. Thought you knew! You guys seem to be so on top of everything and, at least to a certain degree, one step ahead of us. How your friends knew to clear out before we got to their house, I still haven't figured out. At this point, they could be halfway to Harpson by now, so who knows if we'll see them again anytime soon."

She was being kind to us, it was easy to see, somewhat discreetly letting me know my lineage, for whatever reason, but more importantly, giving us peace of mind as to the status of our friends. They weren't dead or even captured.

"Well, they're smart, so I doubt you guys will find them," I said, trying hard to suppress my smile.

"Eh," Geraldine shrugged noncommittally. "Well, good luck in here you two. The blood moon is in another two months, but after that, I imagine we'll probably be a bit more relaxed in our treatment of you, you know, once the danger has passed. Not that we'll let you out of here, but maybe we can allow you some more luxuries. I think it's appalling they haven't even put a divider in your cell to at least partition off the bathroom from the rest of the cell."

"Yea…we just don't look," I said awkwardly.

"Mm," she grunted, shrugging again. "Well, I hope you come to like your new home. Though…well, I guess in a year or so it might not be your home, if we build a new Confinement. You know, when we go to Harpson and the rest of the mainland. We are just too crowded here. I know you saw that space we have with the woods, but there's only so much of that, and we don't want to live in one giant city forever. Plus, I know that we don't have babies frequently, but we still do have them, and they're immortal too. I mean, just look at you!" she said. She was clearly rambling, but I listened carefully, lest I should miss her point. "But at least when we finish preparing our weapons and items for war, we can go and kill all the mortals and take their land. That should give us some more room to spread out for a good long time!"

Her point was not difficult to miss.

There was an awkward pause before Anders said, "Us mortals aren't as easy to kill as you might think."

"Oh, most of us aren't warriors by any stretch of the imagination, and though many of us have highly developed magical abilities, they can't be stretched over a great distance. The only reason we were able to stretch our immortality over all of the Hersotes was in combination and with careful design—each other's spells making them even more powerful together. But, I'm getting away from my main point. We may not be warriors, but we can't be killed. Even the most fearsome mortal can't stop us. They can put up the fight of their life, but ultimately we will end it. Well, thanks for letting me sneak a peek of you two. Good night," she said, and taking her torch, she left, darkness spilling over us as our few lit candles burned near the toilet at the back of our cell.

I heard rather than saw Anders get out of bed and come up next to me. I was still sitting upright, and he leaned over and whispered in my ear, "She was afraid one of the guards might overhear her, so she tried to speak carefully."

"Yes," I whispered back. "That's amazing about Darius, Raela, and James."

"It is," he whispered enthusiastically. "Though it won't prove much good if the Hersotes go to kill all mortals next year or whenever," he said, his tone suddenly serious and a bit angry.

I nodded in the dark, his eyes close to mine. "I don't know why she told us that part if there's nothing we can do," he added.

"We have a year. Perhaps we're supposed to think of something," I responded, optimistic without real cause.

Chapter Seventeen

After our late night visitor, we managed to fall back asleep, waking up presumably the next day, though for us that simply meant the lighting of more candles.

"So," Anders started, his mouth full of crackers as we sat cross-legged on top of his bed after fully waking. "I was thinking you learn magic."

I coughed on my dry cracker, jumping off the bed to grab a sip of juice. Bringing the tart, maroon drink back to the bed with me, I simply said, "Why? I've specifically avoided magic, and you know my reason."

"Yes," he said, his eyes boring into mine as if he could not understand my reluctance. "But," he continued, changing to a whisper, "don't you think we were told about the planned invasion for a reason? The only thing I can think of that we can do from in here is help you learn magic."

"To what end? Plus, you're forgetting, Meraldia has magic—powerful magic. And she lives down the hall!" My voice had risen and Anders frantically shushed me. We both listened quietly for a minute then.

Hearing no interrogative footsteps, Anders calmly continued. "I understand, but who's to say you're not even more powerful? You never bothered learning your type of magic. What if it can break through magical barriers?"

The cracker swallowed, I realized I had been chewing on the inside of my bottom lip as Anders spoke. "All right," I hesitantly agreed. "I see your point. It's a long shot, though."

"I know, but do you have another idea?"

I shook my head.

"Let's start then," he whispered enthusiastically, brushing crumbs from his pants and bedding as he stood. "What do you do first?"

"Um…," I said, following his actions much more slowly as I thought. "Well, ideally I would go away for up to a few months, focusing my energy on things and trying simple spells in an attempt to discover my throsote. The throsote is really necessary and helpful to focus on, especially when you're just starting out. Also, I think beginners usually find a wand helpful as a physical focal point in addition to their throsote....Magic's not easy by the sound of it, but that's really the extent of my knowledge. Since I never wanted to learn, my father really never spoke of it to me. Those are just little details I gleaned from a conversation here or there."

Anders' enthusiasm faded slightly at my vague description of practicing magic. "All right," he finally said, his brow scrunched down in thought. "So, how exactly do you focus your energy on things to find your throsote?"

"I don't really know details, that's the problem. I mean, I guess focusing your energy on particular things with your attention and seeing if something happens?" It came out as a question rather than a statement.

"All right," Anders said again, slowly. "So...are throsotes always natural things, like the moon?"

"I—I'm not sure. I think so."

"And before, you said that they could be passed down?"

"They can, but they aren't always. And if mine is the moon, then we're especially in trouble since that's the thing they're specifically trying to keep me from seeing."

"Well...what was your mom's?"

"Remember, I don't know. I didn't want to know anything about magic. Even my mom's."

Anders nodded his head, and we stood silently for a few minutes. My mind began wandering to my limited memories of my mother's magic. How she swirled falling raindrops in midair until they formed a little ball and my raucous laughter as she stopped and it popped into tiny droplets. Her brushing the hair from my eyes with a flick of her wrist and the kiss of a pleasant breeze. Her dancing with my father near the empty fireplace, her skirt twirling with life in our still, cramped cottage.

"I think...," I began, "my mother's magic had something to do with the wind."

"Great," Anders said, and he quickly whipped the blanket from his bed. Without any other words, he stepped back and began fanning me with it wildly and enthusiastically.

"Wait, wait," I called, the air moving my currently unkempt tangle of loose hair back from my face.

He stopped and looked at me expectantly.

"I think her magic had to do with the wind. That's not necessarily her throsote."

"Well," he said, giving me a half-smile, "it's worth a try." And he went back to fanning me.

I straightened up, took a deep sigh, and tried to focus on the fake wind. I squinted at it, its unevenness making it hard to stare at directly. I tried to clear my thoughts, then I tried to focus on the feeling of the wind on my skin, through my hair, tickling my cheeks, drying my lips.

Nothing.

My concentration was finally broken as I realized that the wind seemed to be coming less consistently. "Take a break, Anders," I said, and he didn't argue as he let the blanket drop. I had most assuredly been having him fan me at top speed for at least fifteen minutes.

"What was your father's type of magic or throsote?" he asked, reaching for the juice jug I had left next to the side of his bed.

"His magic had to do with light. It was really quite beautiful. And I never asked, but I'm fairly certain that his throsote was water."

"There are a couple of containers of water in here," he said, dashing over to our food box.

He pulled out an opaque jug and took a swig before handing it to me and watching my face eagerly. He was so hopeful and unusually energetic in contrast to his more common listener's attitude. I stared into the jug, and could only see a dark reflective surface inside.

"It's hard to see," I started reluctantly.

"Here, pour some into my hands so you can see it," he offered, and I did. The water was clear, reflecting the candlelight in our cell over Ander's cream-colored skin.

I stared at it, watched the ripples, and still nothing happened.

Not deterred, Anders suggested we try fire next, and so I sat for a time staring at a candle flame, watching the light flicker and dance, jump and burn tall. Still nothing happened, and eventually my mind wandered to the outside world. Even if I could learn a type of magic that would free Anders and me, how were we supposed to keep an entire world of mortals safe from a large group of Hersotes? My outlook on our situation slumped in the extreme, and I eventually stopped staring blankly at the candlelight and suggested we take a break from magic.

Around what we assumed was dinnertime, Anders tried to cheer me up as we again sat on top of his bed, the only cushioned surface other than my own bed. "Don't worry. You yourself said that it takes people a few months sometimes to discover their throsote and magic type."

"Yea," I said, staring angrily at the brown cracker before me. I was already sick of crackers.

"And I know we don't have a ton of natural items down here, but maybe if your throsote is, say, wheat…maybe if you focus on a cracker hard enough you could discover it."

It sounded like a joke to my mind, but Anders was not laughing, instead already gazing into my eyes when I looked up into his excited and hopeful ones. I couldn't help myself as the small crack of a smile formed on my lips. "We can keep trying," I said, taking another mouthful of my current cracker.

"So, what do you want to do tonight?" Anders asked, wiping his mouth on his black cotton sleeve.

"I don't know," I said, staring futilely around at the sparse cell.

"We could try telling each other stories."

"Made up or ones that we've heard elsewhere?"
"Either," he said.

"All right," I agreed, my mood already lightened considerably. "You start," I said, popping the last of my chosen crackers for the night into my mouth.

"All right," he said, rubbing his hands together in front of him, seemingly gearing up for an exciting start. "In a distant land, lived a young woman."

"Wait, is this a story you already know, or one you're making up?"

"One I'm making up as I go," he said, and he barely paused before continuing. "This young woman was once a royal princess, but she did not know it, for she had been stolen away from her family shortly after birth. On the run, her captors had died in a horrific storm, but then an old farmer had found the abandoned baby and decided to raise her as his own. Little did he know she was a princess. As she reached adulthood, her adoptive father grew very ill and eventually passed away. As his farm was taken from her after her father's death, she set off on the road, trying to think of a way to make a living. She had always enjoyed dancing, and so that's where she decided to start—living a nomadic life of performing. Stopping at various villages, she would gather the people together in their town squares, twirling in the light of the moon and the twinkling stars. Nothing could compare to her beauty when she danced. She was free and beautiful. Her blonde hair gleamed in the sky's nightlights and her hands danced with her body, delicate yet deliberate in the motions of her fingers. Her green eyes were deep."

Anders was still talking, but my green eyes were focused on his brown ones, which had drawn inexplicably closer to mine.

"She was just beautiful. And brave, even when—no, especially when things around her were just flat-out terrifying. And she can be blunt, but still kind, and—." In mid-sentence, Anders' words stopped as he reached for me, our lips immediately finding each other's. Falling backward with Anders partially on top of me, I reached my arms around his neck as his hands reached into my tangled hair. His mouth was warm, as was his pale skin, his one hand hot through the fabric on my arm.

Still kissing, we shifted slightly, lying sideways with our heads toward the foot of his bed. Suddenly, Anders pulled back very slightly, his brown eyes suddenly opened and looking into mine. "This isn't like with James?" he asked.

I knew the answer at once. "No. It's not like that at all," I stated, and our lips touched once more.

I was elated and excited. Anders' lips broke free from mine then only to move to my neck. A few seconds later, though, he stopped. Something dropped in the pit of my stomach as he slowly moved backward, pushing himself upright as I lay below him on top of his bed.

"What is it?" I asked slowly, his brown eyes looking over and past me. I turned my head to follow his intense gaze and saw nothing out of place—only my own bed, the box of food, and in the far corner, the tub and toilet.

"What is it?" I asked again as I started to sit upright too. But all at once Anders pushed me back down as he jumped backwards off of his bed, moving against the cell wall in apparent fear. His brown eyes looked in my direction but not at me, black and animalistic in terror. His cheeks still appeared flushed in the candlelight, though the rest of his face was pure white against his messy black hair.

Very slowly stepping down off of his bed, I took a tentative step toward him, one hand outstretched in comfort. "Anders, it's me, Sarah," I began, feeling the need to remind him of his surroundings, to pull his consciousness back to the present. "What's wrong?"

His throat constricted as he swallowed. "It's a full moon," he whispered, still staring past me.

I stopped in place for a second, shocked as I realized that he must suddenly be feeling the moon's effects even though we were far from its reaches. I remembered how he said that Slytons were like this, feeling the moon's effects even when he was locked in the darkness of his house. I took another careful step toward him when he screamed, "Get away from me!" His black eyes finally locked on mine, and I jumped backward, my legs hitting the side of his bed as I fell back onto it.

"Stay away," he said, quieter this time but still serious and slightly threatening. "I don't want to hurt you, Sarah."

I nodded quietly, my heart thumping wildly in my chest and my breathing coming in slow, huge gulps. I nervously tucked my hair behind my ears, noticing that Anders' gaze had fallen back to the other side of the cell.

"What are you looking at, Anders?" I asked quietly, still seeing nothing where he looked.

"A door," he said, his voice far-off as if he were not actually talking to me.

"A door," I repeated dumbly, and then a realized. "A door to hell?" I asked, whipping my head around once more to look at nothing.

"I can't go in it. I don't want to go in it," he said, and upon looking back at him I noticed that his fists were clenching the legs of his pants tightly while the ends of his hair dripped with sweat. "I don't want to go in," he repeated. "But...but I do."

I jumped up and ran over to him, holding onto his shoulders, blocking his view of the door that was invisible to me. At my touch he emitted an exhalation of breath that came out very much like a growl. "Get off me," he threatened darkly.

"Anders," I said, not moving my hands, "you can't go in there."

"I—," Anders started, but he immediately cut himself off. "Wait. Yes, I can," and for a moment the muscles in his face relaxed as did his shoulders under my touch. "I can leave and come back to our world through a different door. Out of this cell." And he marched in its direction abruptly, tripping me with his sudden movement so that I fell at his feet. Looking up at him, he turned and spared a glance down at me, his face filled with pain and anguish, before he continued marching quickly toward the other side of our cell.

"Wait!" I called, and surprisingly he stopped and turned toward me. "Let me come with you!"

"You can't," he said, though the words weren't as menacing as some of his others had been. "You don't belong there, so you'd be stuck there. Forever. Just like a mortal who has died."

And he took another step toward the invisible door. "I thought the doors only appeared outside," I said, desperate to keep him with me, afraid of what would happen if he left.

"Not always. Usually, but not always," he said, stopping in his tracks, but not turning to look at me. "Once, several years ago, a door appeared in my room. It had been an especially bad day, and it took everything that I had not to enter the door that night. My…my mother entered a door once. After she and my father had had a fight, before they had me. She managed to find another door in hell, though. She came back out to find him."

"Right away?" I asked.

"It took her three months," he answered. "She said that was extremely fast." And he stepped forward, stopping on his own this time. He turned and looked at me once more, and with his hands outstretched in the direction of his body but with his gaze still on me, he took another step forward. All at once, he disappeared. The candles in the cell all blew out, leaving me in complete darkness, afraid and alone.

Chapter Eighteen

It took what must have been many hours for one of the guards to realize that Anders was missing. The guard had come with another box of food, and after lazily pushing it toward me, peered all around the cell, then bright with many candles that I had found and lit in the dark. I could see the almost comical fear in his eyes as he realized that it was only I who inhabited the cell. Then, without a word to me, he rushed back down the hallway.

In no time at all, I could hear the thudding of several pairs of running feet. And all at once, several women and one man appeared before me, Octavia and Geraldine among them.

"Where is the young man?" Octavia demanded fiercely. "Did you use magic to make him disappear somehow?"

I had been lying in my bed when the guard had arrived to deliver more food. I had sat up at the time, but had not bothered moving any further since.

"He's gone," I said simply, my body and emotions quite numb still from the shock of seeing Anders slip into a door to hell with barely any warning.

"How?" Octavia snapped again, her face growing bright red in her boiling anger.

"He went to hell," I said again, practically monotone.

"What do you—," Octavia started, but she cut herself off as the members of the group took a sharp breath of air, almost in unison. "He was a Slyton," Octavia said quietly to herself and the group, though her focus remained on me. "He was a Slyton?" she screamed then, seemingly directing the question at me.

I nodded mournfully. "And now he's gone."

Octavia was shaking, obviously livid that we had pulled one over on her. Suddenly, taking a deep breath, her shoulders heaving, she stated, "Well, I guess that is one less mouth to feed then." Her shaking had already stopped, I noticed. "As I'm sure you're aware, Slytons are often in hell for years, if they return at all. I can't say I blame him. An eternity in a dark cell with you or an eternity in his true home with his real father and family."

And with those cutting words, she stormed off, Geraldine and the few others following in her wake, not sparing additional glances for me.

I spent what must have been days in anguish. But as I tried to focus on Anders and the good things that had been said and passed between us, I realized that there was still some degree of hope, however small. He had told me, right before he left, that his mother had both entered and left hell. Granted, it had taken her a few months, but she had done it. So Anders could do it too.

Also, I could not rid my mind of Anders' enthusiasm for me learning magic. And so I tried various things. I spent hours staring at the fire from the candles. I tried to focus my energy on our crackers, as silly as this felt, picturing fields golden with wheat where the cracker's ingredients had originated. I stared at my gauzy cotton dress, picturing squeezing newly picked cotton in a field. I lay against the beams of wood on the floor, trying to feel the trees from which they came.

And nothing happened.

I lost complete track of hours, and eventually days. I went to bed when I was tired and awoke when I wasn't. I had little contact with people, only occasionally seeing a guard when they would bring me food and check on the cell.

And though my waking hours were routine enough, spent trying to discover my throsote, my sleep was always filled with terrible nightmares, most of which focused on Anders and his presumed current location. In some dreams, he was searching for a way out, and he could find none. Fire would lick at his pale skin and tears would pour from his eyes. He would scream and beg for mercy, and he was alone. And yet in other dreams, I could see him sneering at the tormented dead there. They screamed in pain and Anders laughed, not bothering to look for a door out because he had found his home.

One night, I awoke suddenly from one of these dreams, my body and bedsheets drenched in sweat. I was breathing hard, glancing at Anders' empty bed automatically to be sure that he wasn't there. Catching my breath, I stared absently before me where I saw a woman standing, silently, in the hall outside of my cell.

"What are you doing there?" I spat, still upset by my dream, though I quickly recognized the woman as Geraldine.

"I just came to pay you a visit and see how you're getting on by yourself. You know it's noon, right? Or have you already lost track of time?"

"I—I just don't care," I said, still somewhat angry from my nightmare.

"Ah," she said.

"How long has Anders been gone?" I then asked.

"About a month. That's what made me think to come pay you a visit actually. There was the first full moon since his departure just last night."

I felt that brief flicker of hope that I tried to keep alive.

"Though to the best of my knowledge no Slyton has ever entered and exited hell so quickly," she said, and though I knew that she was more than likely trying to keep up harsh appearances in case the ears of the guards down the hall should wander, she effectively stepped on that growing glow of hope.

"I know," I said, my voice stuck in my throat, sounding as depressed as I felt.

"Well, the good news is that means the blood moon is only another month away. And then hopefully treatment of you will be a bit nicer. Bye now. Nice talking with you."

I stared at the empty hall where Geraldine had been standing. Eventually, though, I rubbed my eyes. As much as I hated returning to the tortured or hate-filled Anders of my nightmares, I was exhausted, whether or not it was really noon above, under the bright sun.

Chapter Nineteen

I didn't know how many days had passed since my most recent visit from Geraldine, only how many times I had laid down to a restless sleep— nine. I had started to keep track of this at least, with the realization that the blood moon was coming.

On the tenth time I lay my head down, to a dream in which Anders was the tortured instead of the torturer, I was awoken to screams—real screams.

They only lasted a second, the yelled fragment of a word, before they were silenced. I sat up in my bed, very still and oddly terrified as I heard the loud thudding of running footfalls, much the same sound as when Octavia and the others had come to check on Anders' disappearance. As the torchlight swelled and drew nearer in the hall, I looked expectantly at the edge where the people would appear.

The first face I saw—to my happy shock and immediate burst of joyful tears—was Anders'.

"Anders!" I exclaimed, momentarily blind to all potential danger. His usually pale face was flush as it had been the last time I had seen him and his hair was just as knotted. His clothes were different, however; a soft green shirt, emerald in shade, and a crisp pair of brown pants above black, leather shoes.

"Sarah," he said, breathing hard, but clearly happy. "I'm so glad they didn't move you."

Another voice spoke up then, and I reluctantly turned my gaze away from Anders toward its speaker. "Sorry to rush you, but we don't have a lot of time. Please follow these directions exactly." As I surveyed the young adult, male face and the two other male faces behind his, the one speaking threw the end of a rope into my cell. I immediately jumped out of bed and walked toward it as the man explained. "Tie the rope around your body tightly. Then take this," he said, tossing in a small container. I opened it up as he continued to speak. "Swallow that mixture. It will make your heart and other life functions stop entirely. Don't worry. It will only last for ten seconds or so, followed by a deep sleep. These seconds of apparent death is what we will use to pull you from the cell with the rope. It's important that you tie it tightly so that we can pull you out quickly; you know we can't go in after you without becoming trapped ourselves. I nodded and set to work immediately, not caring about the man's identity as he was with Anders.

One of the two other men whispered to the one who had given me instructions, "The spell holding the guards will only last another couple of minutes." I didn't watch his reaction as I finished triple knotting the rope around my middle.

"You may want to take that lying down so you don't fall and hurt yourself," Anders spoke up quickly before I scooped out the mixture with my hand. I nodded, lay down, and licked the grainy substance from my hand. It tasted like vomit, but I managed to swallow it, keeping my focus on Anders' slight smile and deep brown eyes peering down into mine.

Chapter Twenty

Before I even opened my eyes, the light burned at them. I shifted, covering them with my hands, blocking out some of the excruciating sunlight.

"Anders!" a familiar woman's voice called from near at hand. "She's waking up!"

I felt movement at both of my sides.

"Sarah, it's me." I recognized Anders' voice at once.

"And me and Darius," the young woman said, whom I was somewhat surprised to recognize as the voice of Raela, having not seen our other friends since our house in Grotania.

I pulled my hands away from my eyes, but could not bear to open them yet.

"It's all right," Anders said. "Take your time opening your eyes. I know it's a lot to adjust to after being in that cell for so long."

I felt a soothing, delicate hand stroke my own hand, presumably Raela's. "Poor dear," she said.

"We have you in the shade, so hopefully it won't be too bad for you," Darius finally spoke up.

"Where's James?" I mumbled, having not heard his voice.

"He's gone with a group of Lystian soldiers in the large ship we came to rescue you in. They've gone their separate way in the hope of luring any Hersote pursuers away from you," Anders said.

"Why did he do that?" I asked. James volunteering himself to go into a potential battle with a bunch of soldiers did not sound like the nervous, guilty-conscience James who had been preparing for a life as the village school teacher.

"He—he seems to have a good mind for military strategy," Raela said, her voice coming out a little like a strained wheeze. I'm—we're proud of him. It's just a bit nerve-racking."

I nodded, the motion causing the light to dance and pop around my closed eyelids.

I heard a soft thudding noise draw closer. "Is she waking up?" a male voice asked.

"Yes, though she hasn't been able to open her eyes yet," Darius's deep voice responded.

"Other than that, how do you feel, Sarah?" the same male voice asked.

"All right, I think."

"This is Prince Derrick," Anders explained, and I felt a jolt of shock, my eyes blinking open involuntarily before shutting them once more against the light.

"Prince Derrick?" I asked, rubbing at my sore eyes. "Like the prince."

"The same," the voice responded.

"How...why?"

"Well, first James, Darius, and Raela came to us and explained the situation in Grotania, with you being taken prisoner. I wasn't able to gather enough support for a rescue operation at the time because even as Lystians, going up against the Hersotes is tricky business. However, once Anders found us too and explained the Hersotes' plans, it was a bit easier to stage a rescue, especially if you command any sort of power that may be able to help us."

"I'm not sure yet if I can," I said, thinking immediately of my failed attempts to use magic in the jail cell. Though belatedly, a more serious thought hit me; there was a sure way to help the mortals, though that would also mean the end of my own life.

As if reading my thoughts, Prince Derrick continued, "Well, when we reach Harpson, Anders suggested to me that you meet with some of the Lellio advisers who work in my father's court. Perhaps they have ideas on how to manipulate the power within the blood moon in a few weeks."

"The blood moon is in only a few weeks?" I asked, slowly trying to open my eyes, colors and people all a blur before me.

"Just less than a few weeks actually. The wind is currently on our side. If the weather stays with us, we should hopefully be able to reach Harpson in about a week."

"Where are we now?" I asked, the shapes of people slowly coming into focus.

"A tiny island on the way. We stopped to be sure that we weren't being followed. The ship with your friend James and some of the soldiers are heading to the north of Lystia, and it seemed to attract a single ship in response, though I expect more will head to Harpson once they realize that their pursuit of that ship is fruitless."

As if on cue, I saw the blurred outline of another person approach. "Prince Derrick, we see no further pursuers, and Henry does not seem to detect any unnatural magic, so we feel safe to continue in a bit."

"Wonderful," Prince Derrick said, and he moved away, leaving me once again in just the company of my friends.

"How are your eyes?" Anders asked, leaning down close over me.

"Starting to come into focus a bit," I said, his black hair standing out obviously against the pale blur of his skin.

"Just relax, Sarah. Take your time," Raela said, gently pushing a strand of hair from face.

I took a deep breath, and only then did I catch the warm scent of sand and ocean water. I listened then and heard a bird squawking in the background. "You all came for me?"

"Of course," Darius said. "We tried our best ourselves. We couldn't just leave you two. Though Anders' arrival was certainly the main thing to secure the help of the Lystian government. Nothing says 'help us' like the promise of imminent doom with the one hope currently in a Grotanian prison."

"How did you get out so quickly?" I asked, directing my focus and my slowly-clearing vision on Anders. I then felt immediately concerned, for I did not know the story he had used to explain his own escape. My face must have betrayed my immediate regret for Raela piped up.

"It's all right. He's told us everything."

"Yes," Anders assured me. "I told them that I'm a Slyton. I didn't tell anyone else, though. Just our friends."

I nodded, and closed my eyes, intending to give them a brief break. "Good. I'm glad everyone knows now."

"Me too," Anders agreed.

"We're glad too," Raela piped up. "Though I understand Anders wanting to keep it a secret. After the way we…I treated you, finding out that you were immortals."

I blinked my eyes open again and put out my hand. Raela took it, and I squeezed it lightly in reassurance.

We were quiet for a few minutes as I attempted to use my eyes some more. Slowly, I could make out the details I had been missing: the dark circles beneath Anders' eyes, the healthily tanned complexion of Raela's normally fair skin, and the wide shoulders of Darius, his bulk appearing even larger and more intimidating than usual.

"So you've been in Harpson this whole time?" I asked, directing my question at Raela and Darius.

She nodded. "Yes."

"You didn't see Agatha while you were there, did you?"

Raela bit her bottom lip awkwardly, her tan skin instantly turning pale.

"We found out that she and Gregory had, apparently, gone to the Lystian government with concerns immediately after they found out our plan to search for the blood moon at Merendinappa Island," Darius explained.

"We—we know that they might not necessarily have been trying to get us in trouble, per se," Raela continued. "But regardless, I think I'm speaking for all of us when I say that we weren't exactly eager to reach out to them after hearing of this betrayal."

I nodded slowly, my head still lying on what I had realized was a bed of cool sand.

"I still think Gregory put her up to it," Anders said, his teeth slightly clenched. "He was afraid the moment we began to confide in them at the port."

"And that's the reason we were discovered by the Hersotes at Merendinappa," Darius cut in.

"How?" I asked, my breath caught in my throat.

"The Lystians now believe that they had Hersote spies within their military ranks," Darius said. "When news of us searching for the blood moon became a rumor among the soldiers, it is believed that the Hersote spies managed to send a communication of some sort, alerting the people who caught us of our arrival as a potential threat."

I gave my eyes another break. "Did they figure out who the spies were?"

"They're fairly certain," Raela continued. "Two soldiers went missing shortly afterward, whom they're guessing were responsible. And just to be certain, they've had every other soldier perform a cut test."

"A what?"

"They gave each soldier a minor cut," Raela explained uneasily. "If they were immortals, the cut would have presumably healed immediately. They found two immortals among their ranks, though those immortals swore loyalty to Lystia. Still, they agreed to stay under watch to prove their loyalty for the time being."

I did not like that a bit, and upon opening my eyes, I saw that my friends did not seem to care for it either, their own eyes squinting and downcast.

"I was never intending to start any trouble for other good immortals."

"I talked to them," Darius said. "They're good people, and they understood the precaution."

I nodded again, the sand sifting through the back of my hair and gently scratching at my scalp.

"I'd like to try to sit up," I said, and Anders and Darius immediately reached for each of my arms to help pull me into a seated position.

"So how was it?" Darius asked lightly. "Being dead?"

Anders looked appalled, but I laughed lightly. "I'm not exactly sure. I can't remember any of it if that's what you're asking. Ingenious idea, by the way. Who thought of it?"

"One of the Lellios in Harpson," Anders answered. "It was a little scary to try since being temporarily void of life is not something usually desirable, but obviously it worked."

"Thank you," I said, staring into Anders' dark brown eyes first before moving my gaze to Darius and Raela. "Thank you for coming for me."

"Of course," Anders said, and my eyes went back to rest on his.

"I'm glad you made it out," I said, afraid to actually verbalize his true whereabouts even though it was no longer a secret.

He half-laughed. "It's certainly not somewhere I'm anxious to return to. I found another door out at the very next full moon, though, and I believe I may have set some sort of Slyton record for doing so."

"How did you make it out so quickly?" I asked.

"I needed to get back to you," he said sincerely, and for a moment it seemed that there was no one but me and him. Then Darius's awkward throat clearing brought me back to the present.

"So where did you come out?" I asked, trying to be more casual, glancing at the others in an attempt to include them in the conversation.

"Thankfully only a day's journey from Harpson, to the north. I think my sudden appearance frightened an old woman, though, who ran back into her cottage, shrieking all the way."

I couldn't help but laugh at the thought, the others hesitantly joining in.

As our laughter faded, I asked, "So you didn't want to stay there?"

He shook his head. "I mean," he started, grimacing at his memories, "being there was like being under the constant influence of a full moon. There was pain and suffering, and some...some part of me wanted that." He shut his eyes hard and looked down, and I regretted pressing the issue. He looked back up at me then, opening his eyes. "But, like I said, I had someone important to get back to."

I smiled and glanced at the inquisitive face of Raela and the half-smirk on Darius.

"So...what now?"

"Just what Prince Derrick said. Back to Lystia," Darius said, and he stood up, not bothering to brush the dry sand from his pants.

He offered me a hand, and I took it, helped up by Anders and Raela as well. Thankfully, I found that my legs were not particularly weak after only a few moments of standing, and while my eyes needed to adjust all over again after stepping into full sun, I soaked in the feeling of the rays beating against my light hair and prickling over my unnaturally pale skin.

After the small boat launched from our little island stopover, I stood on the deck for a time, which was very similar to the deck on the small boat we had used to find Merendinappa Island. Unlike the beginning awkwardness of that trip, Raela, Darius, and Anders all stayed above deck with me, each of us leaning on the side of the rail, inhaling the salty air and breathing deeply as the waves jostled and rocked us pleasantly toward our home country.

Having no desire to sleep in darkness, we received permission from Prince Derrick (whom I finally saw to be a young man of our age with a very pointed and distinguished nose and an instantly disarming and genuine smile) to sleep on the deck.

That first night, the stars above shimmered playfully, and I slept deeply, knowing that when I would awake, it would be to the sun and not the tiny flame of a candle.

Chapter Twenty-One

"So then after James saw that people were coming for you, you actually climbed down the third-story window from a rope made of bedsheets?" I asked in shocked disbelief. "Weren't you afraid the knots tying them together would come undone?"

"I know I was!" Darius said, and with his large bulk I could completely understand his fear. "That's why we sent Raela first."

She laughed, her bronzed skin highlighting her olive green eyes. "Well, James said something didn't seem right about the group of Hersotes gathering outside, so we just went for it."

"And so we ran further into the city actually, but there weren't really any people out during the night. And then eventually we found the coast with a tiny personal port for some big important person who lived there, I guess. Anyway, we stole a teeny tiny boat and set sail for Lystia. Took us almost two weeks, but we made it thanks to James's good sense of direction."

"Wow. That's a miracle. I'm so glad you guys got out," I said. And while I didn't want to ruin our good mood and openness, I felt compelled to add, "The Hersotes might have killed you. There were rumors of planning to kill Anders before his escape."

Raela and Darius nodded seriously, their jaws set tight.

"Yea, I was really nervous I'd wind up in hell," Anders said, and despite the off-color joke, he succeeded in re-breaking the tension.

I looked upward at the bright blue sky, void of any clouds that day. I breathed deeply. We had been on the ship for three days at that point, and we were making excellent time, expected to arrive at Lystia in less than two more days.

"So, would you mind telling me again about the crackers that you guys played with like small children?" Raela said, her smile having not faded.

"We were bored," Anders said, shrugging good-naturedly.

"Apparently," Darius said, breaking into an uncharacteristic, full-on grin.

"On that note," Anders said, standing abruptly, "I'm hungry. I'm going to go get some fruit. I'm never eating another cracker again."

"I'll come too," Darius said, following his lead. "Bring you girls back anything?"

"Sure," Raela accepted pleasantly.

"Anything but crackers for me too please," I said before they made it to the steps leading below deck where the food was stored, and where I still could not bring myself to go, away from the sun and breeze.

Left alone with Raela, she smiled at me, hugging her knees. "I'm glad you're all right," she said.

"Thanks, Raela." I smiled, feeling for the first time in what seemed like ages that I had my old friend back.

"So…" she began, almost mischievously, peering at me out of the corner of her eye. "You and Anders, huh? When did that start?"

I coughed on my own spit, having not been expecting the question. She laughed at my surprised response, though didn't say anything further as Anders and Darius were already returning, each bearing a few apples.

I had already had seven apples over the last few days, but I couldn't get enough of the sweet juice after all of the powdery crackers.

That night, the captain of our small ship informed us that he expected this to be our last night on the boat. Although we would still have a couple of days' journey to Harpson on foot, it felt like the end of the simple part of the journey to me…and the end of our peace. I would undoubtedly be asked many questions in Harpson, and I did not relish the thought.

Pushing it from my mind that night, I stood at the side of the deck while the others went to sleep not far away. I took deep, soothing breaths, feeling happier and healthier than I had in a long time. My skin was slightly sunburnt, but I didn't care; the sun's ungentle touch was still a vast improvement over the dark claustrophobia of the Confinement.

I was not alone long before I heard the soft approach of footsteps from behind me. As a hand gently touched my back and then moved around my shoulder, wrapping me in one arm, I did not have to look to know it was Anders.

"Beautiful night," he said casually, half-embracing me as he held on to the rail of the ship with me.

"Mm," I hummed in agreement.

He leaned down and kissed the top of my head lightly. I closed my eyes and snuggled into his side further.

We were silent for a long time, staring at the waves cutting peacefully across the sea.

Very quietly, almost hard to hear over the sound of the water against the boat, Anders spoke. "In the Confinement, you told me that our kiss wasn't just a right time, but wrong person thing." I nodded, my head moving into his shoulder, almost a nuzzle. "How did you know? Or, I guess, when did you know?"

I thought for a minute. "I'm not sure. I...I overheard you talking to James one night in the house. He was basically explaining how I wasn't the one for him, but you...you actually seemed to know me. I mean, you do have an unfair advantage, hearing my fears," I jabbed playfully, "but you wanted to know the person behind the fears. It was obvious. And I guess I started to realize, I wanted to know you too. I always tried to keep my distance in the past. Honestly, I was a bit afraid of you because of what you could hear. But the more I talked with you, spent time with you, I realized I actually wanted to open up to you. And our time in the Confinement together just helped me realize it completely. You were someone I could laugh with, even in what seemed a hopeless circumstance. And while words cannot express how happy I am that we are out of there," I said, my voice lowering momentarily in relief, "I was still glad I was sharing that...adventure with you."

He squeezed his arm around me tighter.

"What about you?" I asked.

"When did I know about you? Oh gosh. I mean...well...I guess I've been trying to deny that you were any special part of the group for quite some time. I mean, I could always hear your fears, but I found myself wanting to know more than that. You were always so fun, despite your...heavy past. But like I've told you, I had always planned on finding a mortal girl. So I specifically fought against wanting to know you deeper. Foolish in hindsight. It wasn't really until Celia's death, I guess, that I felt thrust into a sort of partnership with you. And so that's when I finally allowed myself to open up to knowing you deeper. Horrible, non-romantic answer, I know."

"No, I understand," I said, glancing over my shoulder at our two sleeping friends.

I sighed deeply, looking back out at the vast ocean, shimmering playfully beneath the lively night sky. "I'm not looking forward to docking in Lystia."

He grunted. "Me neither." A pause followed. "Sarah, don't let the king or his advisers bully you once we get to Harpson."

"All right," I agreed, turning to look up at his pale, serious face even though he was still staring off at the sea.

"I had to tell them about you to a certain degree and that you may have power that will help destroy the immortals because I needed their help to free you. And it's not a lie—we still haven't explored your powers fully yet in addition to what your bloodline offers. But I didn't come to rescue you so you could die."

I shuddered. "I know. I...there are undoubtedly going to be many difficult decisions to make in the near future. I don't want to die. The thought is absurd, honestly. I've never much considered the idea of dying. But I can't let all of the mortals in the world die either if I have the power to stop it. But doing it the way Meraldia set it up...it's suicide."

Anders simply grunted briefly, but angrily.

"Well, we still have a few days until we arrive," I said, and we dropped the subject.

Chapter Twenty-Two

My eyesight was entirely back to normal as we stepped through the city gates at Harpson. Prince Derrick walked before us, protected on each side by the small group of soldiers who had been with us on the rescue journey.

In sharp contrast to Grotania, the city walls and the castle itself stood out in dark gray, imposing stone, quite melancholy in appearance. And truthfully, although they were my protectors and rescuers, I felt a similar feeling of foreboding entering this city as I had the cheerful-in-appearance Hersote one.

Walking through the main castle doors, Anders on my one side, Darius on the other, and Raela next to him, I automatically found myself longing for the sun as it left my back. The castle was cool in the dimly-lit Great Entrance, and as the large oak door swung shut behind us, I felt the insane impulse to pry it back open and run away screaming. Anders took my hand and gave it a comforting squeeze, and I knew not whether he simply expected this reaction after my time in the Confinement, if he were hearing my fears through his power, or if he too were even perhaps having similar feelings from his own time in the Confinement.

Our small group stood there for less than a minute when a slim man in royal purple pants and shirt with a black vest strode out of a side door. "Prince Derrick! Welcome back! I trust the journey was successful. We've all been quite anxious!"

"Yes, yes, Orason. May I introduce you to Sarah," Prince Derrick said, stepping back and gesturing toward me with a flourish of his hand.

"Sarah, the unique Hersote," this man, Orason, said, walking toward me with an exaggerated walk of great strides in his excitement. "A pleasure to meet you, miss. I'm Orason, the Prince's main adviser and, if I may be so bold, organizer of his life."

Prince Derrick laughed, his one eyebrow rising playfully and giving his wrinkle-free face a look of extreme youthfulness. "I'll allow it."

"So you're probably starved. We'll prepare something for you in the kitchen. In the meantime, King Edward has requested your immediate presence upon your return."

"Of course," Prince Derrick said. "The throne room then?"

"Yes," said Orason, and he hurried back through the side door whence he came.

"Right through here then," Prince Derrick said, comfortably leading the way toward the huge double doors directly in front of us, surrounded on either side by a double staircase.

Prince Derrick simply nodded at the two soldiers stationed on each side of the wooden doors, and they were opened quite quickly for us despite their size and apparent weight.

"Father, we've returned!" Prince Derrick jovially announced, his voice echoing in the cavernous room before us. It was void of any furniture except for two thrones at the far end, one filled by a robust king and another, slightly smaller one to his right-hand side, presumably for Prince Derrick. Bright red and purple tapestries hung on the walls, absorbing some of the echoes, but not enough to stop our arrival from seeming quite thunderous with our out-of-sync footfalls.

I had only ever seen pictures of King Edward, and the reality was not quite as regal as I had been expecting. His voluptuous stomach poured over his too-tight pants as he sat, spread-legged on his throne. His face was bright red as if recently angered, and I once again felt the impulse to turn and run away. Thankfully, Anders was still holding my hand and gave it another reassuring squeeze.

"Glad you're back," the king said gruffly. Upon reaching his throne, the soldiers around me knelt, and so my friends and I awkwardly followed suit as Prince Derrick merely bowed his head at his father.

"Father, may I present Sarah, the Hersote." I hated this new attachment to my name, as I had not related at all to the Hersotes in Grotania, and only vaguely recognized myself as one. Nevertheless, on this cue, I stood up, the others hesitantly following my lead while making room for me to pass through to the front of the group. I relinquished Anders' hand quite reluctantly.

"Sarah, welcome back to Lystia," the king said, tugging on his fully gray, wiry beard. The solid gold crown atop his head was massive, even on his overly large head. "When your friend, Anders, informed us of the Hersotes' plans, we obviously wanted to do everything within our power to free you. You are, as I'm sure you're aware, our only reasonable hope. I have spent many hours meeting with my Lellio advisers. They are powerful—the most powerful in the country—but they can only do so much against a foe who cannot be killed. Rumor has it, though, that you can not only level the playing field, but demolish it. So, we know they wish to attack us at some point in the near future. What can you tell me other than that?"

"Truthfully, not much. I only know that they've been preparing for it. Whether this is just through the construction of actual weapons or through magical preparation, I can't say. The Hersotes…time is nothing for them, you understand. So either way, I doubt their intent is to kill all mortals in the blink of an eye. Nevertheless, if they somehow manage that capability, I'm sure they would use it."

"Right," the king said, wiping a large, plump hand over his oily face. "And so, more importantly, what can you tell me of your own powers?"

I went into as much detail as I could about our brief meeting with my great-great-grandmother and her words recorded in the magical stone.

"Perfect!" the king said, cutting me off quite abruptly when I explained that practically my mere presence in the moonlight on the night of the blood moon would kill off the Hersotes everywhere.

"Well…I mean, that is perfect, but it also means I would die," I said, trying to be brave.
The king grimaced and his lip raised in a sneer for the fraction of a second. "And that's a sacrifice you're willing to make, I expect, for the good of your country?"

The sound of silence seemed to echo around the room.

"I mean, it's not a thought I relish, but—but perhaps there is a different way."

"How? Through your own magic?" the king spat at me.

"I, most unfortunately, never discovered my own type of magic or my throsote. I do have another bloodline that may be of interest to you, though," I said, my heart beating wildly. I felt as if I stood in front of an angry criminal court as opposed to the king who had recently sent a detachment to secure my freedom. "You see, while in Grotania, I discovered that I am also the direct descendent of another of the Twelve, Margaret. Her power is the power of combination and her throsote is the moon, which is why the spell of immortality was placed there for safe-keeping."

"And how exactly is that going to help us?"

"Well, I was thinking that maybe I could consult with your Lellio advisers and see if there's anything useful in that."

"That's your plan? You've never even wielded magic of your own and you expect to meddle in the magic of others? I will not leave this up to chance and a vaguely developed hunch. How—how do you even know that this Margerie woman is your grandmother?"

"Great-great-grandmother, your majesty. Another one of the Twelve told me."

"Well then that information can't even be trusted!" his voice boomed.

"Well, this other woman, we believe, was trying to help us with information. She's the one—."

"I've had enough! Are you going to help us all by sacrificing yourself and the evil Hersotes or not?" the king demanded.

His last words echoed around the hall awkwardly, bouncing from floor to ceiling.

"With all due respect, your majesty, I would at least like the chance to speak to your Lellio—."

"I've had enough! Throw her in the prison. If she won't volunteer her life, then we can always take her out on the night of the blood moon and take it!"

"No!" Anders and Raela screamed in near-unison as the soldiers immediately grabbed my arms.

Even Prince Derrick's voice was panicked as he stepped between me and his still-seated father. "Father, if you please, we did not embark on a most dangerous journey of rescue to simply dismiss—."

"It's all of our lives," King Edward growled at his son. "Take her away," he then said to the soldiers. "And get these other people out of my sight."

"Where your majesty?" piped up one of the remaining soldiers as I was turned around, half-drug from the throne room, my feet tripping over each other in my well-worn brown shoes.

"I don't care. Just throw them out of the castle," the king said at my back as the throne room doors opened in front of me.

Before I knew it, I was once more out of the castle and in the bright sunlight. People in the street stopped and stared as I was dragged the short distance from the castle entrance to the city gates. There, the soldiers kept a steady grip on my arms, but moved with a bit less haste as they made a left along a road.

"Where are we going?" I asked after a few minutes, trying to turn my neck to look for my friends, but without success.

"To the jail," one of the soldiers said. The sun was high in the sky at this point.

"Where is the jail?" I asked. I looked all around me at the immediate thinning of dwellings and the green rolling hills before me with little clusters of farms here and there, reminding me of my home village.

"It's only a few more minutes ahead on the right," the soldier on my right explained, almost pleasantly. While I didn't know anything about these soldiers, we had, after all, spent about a week traveling together following their daring rescue of me. This new role reversal was presumably confusing for them as well.

"Why is the prison out here?" I asked as we eventually neared a hill with a cellar door cut out of it.

"Safer to keep our prisoners out here than within Harpson's walls," the soldier holding my left arm said.

This same soldier then released my arm and set to work unlocking the slanted door opening into the ground under the green, grassy hill. The soldier swung the door open wide and then grabbed hold of my arm once more. It was at this point that my feet refused to move, and so the two soldiers half-carried me down the steps into the prison. It was pitch-black at first, but the soldier from my left quickly lit a torch. I saw three divided cells then, iron bars separating them from each other and the outside corridor. I was thrust into one, the gate immediately locked behind me with a traditional lock. Unlike the Confinement's invisible barrier, it was easy to see that I was caged without an escape.

The two soldiers then walked back up the steps, leaving me in the light of one large torch placed on the far wall outside of the cells.

I couldn't see the actual fiery orb from the angle of my cell, but I craned my neck to catch the last rays of sunlight filtering belowground before the door slammed shut.

Chapter Twenty-Three

I was shaking violently, my eyes darting desperately this way and that like a wild animal. There was nothing to look at, though, save a basin that was presumably for the alleviation of one's bowels. I simply sat in the middle of my cell, the packed earth floor cold beneath me. I grabbed my knees and rocked myself back and forth, my eyes remaining wide open the entire time.

Time. I could not lose track of time again without the sun. I started counting. 1, 2, 3, 4, 5, 6. Around 1,000, I burst into tears. I could not do this again. I could not. I glanced frantically around my cell, stood and flung the basin at the bars, which came crashing apart in a rain of ceramic.

"It's all right," I actually said to myself, sitting back down on the cold earth, a jagged piece of ceramic pressing against my bottom unpleasantly, though I didn't bother to move it. "I'll be dead in the blood moon in a week anyway." And I swallowed vomit as part of me was repulsed by the thought that I was actually excited for the blood moon now, for at least I would be in the open air one last time.

There was a terrible squeaking of hinges then as the jail door was opened. Awkwardly, the same man I had met at the castle, Orason, descended the jail stairs, his extreme swagger completely absent in his tiny, timid steps.

"I've brought you a meal," he said, and he slid it beneath the small space between the bars and the floor. Although it appeared to be a fine meal indeed, roasted chicken, potatoes, and jam on toast, I didn't move for it. I simply followed Orason with my eyes, returning to my wild animal role.

Under my violent gaze, Orason quickly made his exit, tripping up the stairs briefly in his flight. And the sun's indirect rays were gone from me once more.

Angered at my loss all over again and that I had not savored the obviously orange rays more, I stood and threw my food tray against the bars this time. Food splattered all around my jail cell and through the bars, though the tray did not smash into pieces. I screamed in anger then for minutes on end. I screamed until my voice was hoarse and cracked, and I once more sunk into a hunched position, closing my eyes and unwillingly embracing the darkness.

I was about to start counting again when the thought hit me—surely Anders, Darius, and Raela would come for me. After all, they were not contained in the cells next to me. So perhaps I would be freed.

And so I found myself repeating over and over again in a hoarse whisper, "They'll come for me."

My mind unwilling to sleep but my body beginning to demand it, I found that my tight grip on my drawn-up knees had slackened. My head had tilted to rest on them and my right shoulder. My stomach growled at me loudly, and I considered picking some of my cold meal from the ground. As I was debating this, though, I jumped as the jail door above opened again.

"They've come for me," I whispered to myself sternly, standing up and holding on to the edge of the cell bars.

As the person's face came into focus before mine, I was at first taken aback, for it was the straight nose and disarming wide eyes and childish, soft lips of Prince Derrick.

Behind him, though, I quickly saw Anders and Darius appear.

"You came!" I shouted, though Prince Derrick's presence quickly spoke against my inner-certainty.

"Of course," Prince Derrick said, pulling a key from within his pocket. "And apparently I came not a second too late, as I'm guessing Anders and Darius were already preparing their own jailbreak." He then smirked in a friendly way. "Just down the road, I found Darius here holding a dagger and Anders holding a jar of spiders and a jar with a snake in it. Any chance you'd like to explain, because they certainly didn't."

I looked at their faces. Anders' cheeks were bright red and he playfully rolled his eyes at me. Presumably fears of the guards he was hoping to exploit, I guessed that I would have found his version of a rescue somewhat comical. Darius's expertise in weapons may have quickly ended any hilarity, however, and his clamped jaw and narrowed eyes behind Prince Derrick seemed to confirm this suspicion.

"So," Prince Derrick continued talking as he unlocked my door and swung the bars open wide, "welcome back to your freedom. I didn't go all the way to Grotania to simply lock you up in your home country." There was an edge to his voice.

"What about your father?" I asked, my voice husky, and I caught the surprised raised eyebrows of all three men in hearing it.

"Well, I doubt he'll lock me in the jail. Though I may make myself scarce until we all die."

"You—you're not expecting me to help you?"

"Come on upstairs," he said first, leading the way. Though still dark aboveground, I was pleased to see instead of torches thousands of twinkling stars and an ever-growing moon lighting the plush green grass on the hills around us. Lights were still on in the houses in the distance and I could hear lively chatter and neighborly merriment drifting toward us.

The guards nowhere in sight, Prince Derrick turned toward me. "I don't expect you to help us any longer. Not after the way that my father treated you. And I certainly don't expect you to be essentially executed after not committing any crime. You were born into a horrible fate—an ironic immortal life almost destined for an early death."

I shuddered. Life of blood, it drips to you.

"I feel for you and the situation in which you find yourself," Prince Derrick continued. "You're free," he abruptly finished, and he began walking back down the dirt road to the left, toward the city gates. On the right was the road that would lead us home, past the little farmhouses where neighbors were still calling to each other, presumably with no idea that their lives would be warred upon in the near future. A note of lively singing rose up in the distance and I caught the playful tune of a fiddle in response.

I could feel Anders and Darius's eyes resting on my back, though I did not move yet to look at them.

As I saw Raela emerge from some bushes to my right where she must have been lying in wait, I turned toward the slowly departing figure of Prince Derrick. "Wait!" I shouted, and he slowly turned around as I raced toward him, my friends following closely behind. "Let me speak to your father once more."

"I don't know that I can rescue you quite as easily next time." Prince Derrick said, his boyish cheeks squishing against his eyes in a half-wince.

"I know."

And silently, almost like a funeral procession, we all returned to the castle.

Chapter Twenty-Four

"I didn't ask you to bring her to me!" the king said in his throne room, angered at having been brought down at such a late hour.

Two guards held my arms for dramatic effect under the direction of Prince Derrick, as if I had been their prisoner the whole way from the jail.

"Father, just listen. I think you'll be pleased," he said, though in truth we had not spoken a word on our return to the castle.

"King Edward," I began, giving as much of a curtsy as I could with my arms held tightly by the soldiers. "Let me start by apologizing. Our meeting earlier obviously did not go as you had expected."

He snorted loudly in response.

"But," I continued, not deterred by his less than gracious attitude toward me, "let me assure you that I would like—no, I need to help my fellow Lystians who would otherwise die at the heartlessness of the Hersotes." I hoped that my rhetoric would appease the king, who unfortunately looked only slightly mollified as his shoulders relaxed almost imperceptibly.

Here was the tricky part—hoping I could make it through my explanation without being interrupted.

"With your blessing, Your Majesty, I would like your permission to at least consult with your Lellio advisers to determine if there is a way to save the lives of the good Hersotes who proudly call Lystia their home. I'm certain that I am not the only immortal within your borders, and the borders of other peaceful countries, who would certainly be affected by such a mass slaughter through the magic of the blood moon."

King Edward opened his mouth to speak, but I kept talking.

"But," I said loudly, "if we discover that nothing can be done, I will proudly sacrifice my life for my country and for those kind people undeserving of such a fate as the Hersotes have deemed fit for them."

The king appeared to be chewing as he considered my words. "You will kill yourself if necessary."

"I will," I said.

He groaned and sighed audibly, his pants appearing as if they would rip at any second if he sat any more spread-legged. "Fine. You can talk with my Lellio advisers, though I don't know what good it will do if you don't know how to use any sort of magic." He then far too belatedly tried to assume an expected kingly air, sitting up a bit straighter and pulling his legs together. "Lystia thanks you for your prepared sacrifice for your country."

I simply nodded in response and turned to walk out before he could throw me in the jail again, the guards awkwardly relinquishing their grasp as I led the way from the throne room.

Orason was waiting for us, changed into simple, but well-made, all black cotton clothes.

"Sarah, so good to see you out of the jail and free again," he said, some of his previous swagger evident in his voice.

"Well done," Prince Derrick said as the throne room doors shut behind us. "For now, I'm guessing you'd just like some sleep. We have guest rooms in the south wing."

Orason snapped into action, leading us up the stairs and down the right side of the hall. Twisting and turning many times and climbing one other smaller flight of dark stone stairs, we arrived in a hall with doors on one side and more red and purple tapestries on the other.

"You may choose which room each of you would like—they've all been readied for your arrival," Orason said, indicating four consecutive doors in turn.

"Thank you," I accepted.

"Of course. I will be staying here at the end of the hall, so please do not hesitate to summon me if you need anything," he said, and he strode away, making sure we were watching to see which door he was entering.

Left alone in the dark hall, a single torch burning, Anders immediately asked, "You're not really going to kill yourself?"

"I—I meant what I said," I replied, not breaking eye contact with Anders, though my eyes felt heavy and sad.

"You can't," he said, and his Adam's apple bobbed, abnormally noticeable.

"I can't let everyone we know, including you two," I said, looking at

Darius and Raela, their own eyes heavy with yet unshed tears, "die because of the Hersotes." I swallowed hard against my still-hoarse voice. "Still, I'm not going down without a fight."

They each nodded silently, Anders squinting in apparent pain, Darius's lips protruded in thought, and Raela's healthy tan once more temporarily faded to white.

"Good night," I said, and I opened the door nearest us and walked inside. I breathed heavily, leaning up against my closed door. The moonlight poured inside the open window of my new room, its cool rays passing through the sheer white netting surrounding the canopy bed. I slowly made my way over to it and climbed inside, shutting the netting around me without shutting out the light. I needed sleep, and while I still needed Anders and my friends, I needed a minute to process my own thoughts. Sleep overtook me before I could think further, though, lulling me into instant security with the scents of warm, late summer grass and distant sheep.

Chapter Twenty-Five

The sun's pleasant burning of my face woke me, and for a moment, my time in jail the day before seemed a bad dream.

I groggily noticed that my sparsely decorated, but well-maintained and clean room had a standing mirror in the corner, near the door, and I went and stood before it. I gasped as I saw my reflection staring back at me; my hair was visibly knotted in some places, dusty in appearance where my hair was normally a lighter shade of blonde than it then appeared. My brown dress was dark from the grime of travel again, seemingly stained in portions where I had sweat. It had been a long time since I had had a proper bath, I realized, and I suddenly longed to clean myself as if nothing else mattered.

Miraculously, as if reading my thoughts, there was a knock on the door. I opened it and found Orason standing there, decked out in purple with gold buttons, his hair combed back sleekly. "Good morning, Sarah. I didn't wake you, I hope?"

"No, no. Good morning, Orason."

He smiled pleasantly, a kind, yet practiced smile. "I didn't know if you'd like it, but I've sent for tubs and clean clothes for you and your companions." He stood back, allowing two servants bearing a large tub full of water, a third servant carrying a neatly stacked pile of clothes, and a fourth servant carrying a tray of steaming food to walk forward.

I immediately jumped back to allow them to pass. "Oh, Orason, thank you so much! You've read my mind!"

He smiled again. "Wonderful. I'll see you later then." And they all departed silently, their heads straight, but not held high, with cheery glances in my direction.

As soon as they had left, I stripped myself of my dress, finding that I actually had dirt caked on various parts of my body, around my ankles and just under the neck of my dress as well.

Without pausing to check the temperature of the tub, I jumped in. It was a bit on the cool side, but I didn't care at all, sighing audibly as I leaned back to allow my hair and entire body to soak in its relaxing waters.

I stayed in the water until my fingertips were shriveled like I had never seen them before. The water around me was cold and dirty, and yet I still removed myself somewhat begrudgingly.

Walking over to the mirror once more, I found my newly washed naked body to be almost as shocking as my previously grimy body. I was pale—extremely so, where my dress had been. And yet my face, arms, and neck stood out red from the sun. My blonde hair was still darker than usual from being wet, though I could already tell that it would take on a lighter dirty blonde hue in just a bit. Almost with dread, I walked over to the small table where the servant had placed the stack of clean clothes; there was something so freeing about having that miserable piece of brown cloth finally from my body.

Lifting the dress, I saw that it was of a pale pink, thick satin material with a floor-length skirt portion. It had rouched lace around the collar and long, soft lace around the three-quarter length sleeves. It was arguably pretty, but not my usual style at all. Nevertheless, I put it on, noticing that it hid all of the noticeable burn lines around my sensitive skin. I then picked up a comb from the bottom of the stack, which sat atop clunky black shoes. Putting on the shoes and stepping in front of the mirror, I combed my hair, which had grown to more than halfway down my back. It was stick-straight while wet, once I untangled the copious knots from it. After this laborious process, though, it already began to bounce with a bit of life as the warm air began to dry it, its look of health returning despite some frizzy patches that persisted from my rough treatment of it the last few months.

I then walked over to the table once more and scarfed down the breakfast that had been left for me, completely cold by that point, but still delicious. Brushing my teeth with the plant remnants left for that purpose, I walked back to the standing mirror.

With a final look at the finished product, I barely recognized myself. Still, I could not help but be pleased with the ultimate result, as I looked much healthier and more radiant than I surely had at any time in the recent past.

And so I swung the door to my room open wide with confidence, and nearly collided with Anders, Darius, and Raela.

"Good morning," they all said, practically in unison, and my smile and light laughter did something to dispel any feelings of unrest I surely left them with the night before.

Like me, they too were washed and dressed in clothing not their own. Darius wore deep green and black, the dark colors accentuating his large size. Raela and Anders, on the other hand, had been given pale blue and white clothes, nearly matching in color. Anders' skin was just as pale as always and his black mop of hair, which had grown to nearly his shoulders, just as dark. On the other hand, the light colors accentuated Raela's tan and gave me a bit of a start as I realized that Raela had presumably not been out of her mourning dress until now.

"So...," Anders began, much more at ease than he had been the previous night, "time to meet with the Lellio advisers?"

"Of course," I said, and we marched off as a group.

Chapter Twenty-Six

A dark gray castle wall surrounded us on all sides in a perfect circle, though the castle courtyard felt far from enclosed. The sky above us was bright blue and out of the bright green, thick grass grew many varieties of flowers and even a few trees. Vines with bright blue blooms climbed the wall in several sections, blocking some portions of the stone entirely.

Similar to the circle of thrones at Merendinappa Island, toward the center of the courtyard and spaced several feet apart from each other, stood seven dark wood seats with high backs.

I stood in the center of the group of chairs with my friends, each of the chairs filled with a different royal Lellio adviser.

The one closest to the courtyard door looked the youngest, not much older than us. Continuing counterclockwise around the circle, the men seemed to be getting older, eventually finding an apparently ancient gentleman with deep canyons of wrinkles in his saggy face and a long gray-white wiry beard.

I felt winded, having just explained my tale as fully as possible to the group.

"So," one of the middle-aged advisers with half-moon spectacles like my father began, "what you're hoping to find is a way of exploiting your blood heritage with this twelfth woman, Margaret, to somehow stop Meraldia's curse, as you might call it?"

"Yes, but specifically it needs to be in a way so that all mortals are not able to be conquered by a foe that cannot die."

"So that they can be killed through a specific type of magic or something?" this same adviser asked.

I took a deep breath. "Actually, I was hoping to make the Hersotes mortals once more. Then the Lystian army and the rest of the world should have a fighting chance."

Several of the advisers exchanged looks before the same adviser, seemingly a spokesman for the group, continued, "You're hoping to change the fate of an entire group of people?"

"I believe allowing us to die through the blood moon would change that fate even more," I said.

He nodded thoughtfully. "I personally believe it can be done," he finally said. "Blood magic is unique and very rare. You see, you said you believe your mother had a sort of wind magic. Let's just say she had conjured a fast wind to move past your house. The wind moves by and that's it—the magic disperses. She didn't store the wind anywhere, and so you have no access to it. But the fact that they had to store this spell in a throsote given that it's a combination of many people's spells, that makes it unique and grants you a certain level of access."

"But it's still only open to her on the blood moon?" Raela asked, and I was thankful for the question, a possibility I myself had not yet considered.

"I would think so. After all, this Margaret woman didn't leave it open because that would make it weak. However, Meraldia's secret ingredient …that specifically leaves it open during a blood moon."

"So, you're suggesting that she pull Margaret's combination magic down from the spell?" a slightly younger adviser with hair the color of mud asked.

"I would think so," the first answered. "You see," he continued, looking at me, "while combination may not be your type of magic, you should be able to use the power that runs through your blood to call it out. You don't have much hope of manipulating it further, but the simple task of pulling it out of the immortality spell in the moon should not be an issue. Once that happens, the other magic should disperse. You would have to do it quickly, though, before Meraldia's separate piece can strike."

"But what would be the effects when it disperses?" the youngest adviser asked, his hand propping up his chin in thought.

"I would think," began the oldest adviser, located to his left and completing the circle, "that it might either drift away, like in the wind example, or the different ingredients could hit some people, either way not causing any harm. Let's say someone is hit with the ability to breathe when breathing is impossible—unless they're currently being choked they probably wouldn't even notice. And in any case, the effects would be temporary like they would ordinarily have been if cast by one of the single twelve."

"So that would make the Hersotes mortal?" I asked, growing excited.

"Yes," the oldest spoke up again. "I would say it would, as it would uncombine the magical ingredients, making them powerful, though still arguably ordinary spells. It's the combination of them that made them more than they are."

"I'm still surprised that the aging of the Hersotes was stopped through a mind power type of magic," the second youngest adviser piped up, scribbling hastily in a thick book as we talked. "We had always guessed it was a more specific anti-aging spell."

Half-Moon Spectacles spoke again, looking me in the eyes as he explained, "We had always guessed, but had not been certain of the twelve types of magic the Hersotes used to create immortality. Don't worry, though," he added, for a look of concern must have been present on my face. "We have no intention of making ourselves immortal. Our interest is purely academic, as we find immortality obviously unnatural, and to a certain degree, evil. My apologies if you find this offensive."

I shook my head in awkward understanding as the young man recording things spoke, still writing, "Plus, the odds of finding magic users who were powerful on their own with all of these specific types of magic would be incredibly low. The Hersotes really lucked out. Any type of mind power magic is exceedingly rare, as is rhythm magic and combination. Consciousness and life overcoming sure-death aren't exactly common either."

I nodded.

"So anyway," Half-Moon Spectacles continued, "you won't need to know your type of magic since you'll simply be tugging on your relative's magic, but you will need to know your throsote in order to release it in the first place."

A ball of dread dropped heavily in my stomach. "I don't know my throsote, though."

"Yes, you've mentioned this, but you have to hope that you can find it before the blood moon. You have a week. It doesn't usually take longer than that."

"Still cutting it close," an older adviser said under his breath.

"Okay," I said, taking deep, deliberate breaths. "So if I discover my throsote, I channel my thoughts and the magic through it and pull Margaret's combination out of the mix?" I asked uneasily.

"Yes," Half-Moon Spectacles simply confirmed.

Thankfully, the youngest adviser came to my rescue with a bit more of an explanation. "Since you've never actually performed magic yet, you should know that it's all about visuals. Magic words and spells are only helpful in conjuring a clear direction and visual for the caster. So you know that you're trying to access combination. Maybe picture Margaret casting it. Picture the spells swirling together, bound through a power. Picture that power being broken and coming toward you, releasing the other spells. And in your mind's eye, cycle that power through your throsote maybe. When you become more skilled, you don't have to necessarily run magic through your throsote, but it should always be in the back of your mind."

I nodded, having turned my whole body to face this helpful man.

"So, if I were you," Half-Moon Spectacles continued, "I'd busy myself with discovering your throsote immediately."

"One thing bothers me, though," the youngest adviser spoke up again, and all eyes turned questioningly toward him. "Meraldia's curse."

Half-Moon Spectacles sighed irritably. "The curse won't matter if she can make the Hersotes mortal first, Gillan. Remember the words? Send to every corner, death for those who wait forever? It's specifically for people who wait forever. So if she's not waiting forever, then it shouldn't affect her, or any other mortal Hersotes for that matter."

"That's not what's concerning me," the young man, Gillan, continued, not unnerved by Half-Moon Spectacles' patronizing tone. "It's the fact that the curse is not specifically for Hersotes."

"How is it not? It's for immortals!" Half-Moon Spectacles countered, though as soon as he spoke the words, his mouth fell at the implication. "Oh. I see," he said.

The meaning had not passed me by either, and I stole a quick glance at Anders, his face especially pale. Raela and Darius were looking at him out of the corners of their eyes too.

"Obviously it would no longer affect the Hersotes if Sarah can perform her part, though there are still immortal Slytons who might be dramatically affected," Gillan said seriously.

"Well," Half-Moon Spectacles drew out the word, sighing deeply. I found my head swiveling non-stop between these two speakers, sitting on near opposite sides of the circle from one another. Half-Moon Spectacles sighed a second time before continuing. "The Slytons are mostly evil.

Perhaps we should simply thank Meraldia and count our victories."

Raela gasped audibly at his words and I felt my face grow tingly. The advisers all looked at us with expressions ranging from concern to mild confusion. "Is there a problem?" Half-Moon Spectacles asked, looking at each of us.

"It's just—is there a way that pulling the combination part out of the spell could maybe make the Slytons mortal too?" I croaked.

"Of course not," Half-Moon Spectacles said, almost laughing. "That part was designed only for the Hersotes. Everyone agrees?" he asked, scanning the faces of the other advisers who nodded in approval.

"Well then, is there a way of altering Meraldia's curse? You know, through blood magic?" I asked.

"To do what?"

"Make the Slytons mortal too instead of killing them outright?" My heart was pounding so hard I would not have been surprised if it's thumping were visibly moving the pink dress fabric against my chest.

Half-Moon Spectacles raised one eyebrow quizzically, half-amused, half-exasperated. "Sarah, why this intense concern for the Slytons?"

"I'm in love with one," I said simply, only belatedly realizing that Anders and I had not professed this deep emotion for one another. Turning to look at Anders, though, he did not look uncomfortable by my words; in truth, he looked so frightened that I would have been surprised if he had heard them at all. Darius and Raela were also staring at Anders, their gazes quite direct and obvious.

Turning back toward Half-Moon Spectacles, he too was staring at Anders. "Ah," he said simply, pulling uncomfortably at his fingers. The other advisers were looking at Anders too, mostly with pitying expressions characterized by drawn, generally bushy, eyebrows.

"So…you're obviously not keen on sacrificing the Slytons," Gillan said slowly.

"No," I said, turning toward him, my hands clasped together, imploring in this involuntary action.

"I can think of two possibilities," he continued, his eyes far-off, and I wondered if he were still formulating his ideas as he spoke. "First, you pull combination out before Meraldia's bit can bleed from the moon."

"That's impossible! As soon as the moon on Merendinappa Island turned red it began to bleed that part of the spell, right Sarah?" Half-Moon

Spectacles demanded, and I hated to confirm this, but I had to.

"See, Gillan!" Half-Moon Spectacles declared. "That'd be impossible, especially for a woman who will be trying magic as something new! She'd have to be lightning fast, so unless she discovers that she is able to wield lightning magic, that seems out of the question."

Gillan did not seem to be listening to Half-Moon Spectacles' obnoxious words. "My second idea is a bit more outside the box. If you could help me in perfecting it," he said, turning to look at his fellow advisers. "Meraldia's curse, as I suppose we're calling it now, should only work if it's just as powerful as the original spell of immortality. That means it will have had to have borrowed that spell's strength, right?"

Slow nods of thoughtful agreement followed from the other advisers.

"You see, Meraldia's curse only needs two things—her actual curse stopping all cycles immediately and the general power strong enough to affect an entire group of people. This power was derived from the combination of all of the spells put together. So the combination part is in there, for sure, but it's not standing out as a key ingredient to Meraldia's curse. So, unlike the immortality spell in the blood moon, pulling out the magic of combination isn't going to disperse the whole spell, just make it weaker because you're reducing some of the magic."

"I agree, Gillan," the man taking notes spoke. "But why not focus her efforts immediately on Meraldia's curse since that's blood magic too?"

"Even as blood magic, she can't manipulate or change it too much. She could only be expected to take out the curse entirely, and then you're left with the power from the immortality spell. Left alone, it might keep the Hersotes immortal, destroying any efforts made from the destruction of the spell in the blood moon," said one of the older advisers.

"Exactly," said Gillan, a smile spreading across his face. "However, she can take out the combination part, weakening the curse's power. Then she can use Meraldia's blood magic to focus on using that weaker power to merely stop the eternal aspect of the curse. Do you all agree that stopping this one small, but obviously crucial detail is possible purely through blood magic?"

Silence followed as the other advisers mentally chewed on Gillan's words. Finally, the oldest spoke, "I believe that it can be. After all, that would not truly change the curse at all, only help to give it a sharper focus as a weaker form of the original curse. This would be very similar to Sarah focusing on killing all Hersotes with the previous curse."

Gillan's large smile and brightened features spoke of victory. "So she uses the weaker curse to actually make them all—Hersotes and Slytons alike—mortal."

"What of the spell in the blood moon?" the note-taker asked, still not looking up.

"The leftover magic disperses as it's inconsequential—just like it would be if all of the Hersotes died from Meraldia's curse. We have to assume that the curse and its borrowed power outdoes any immortality magic still in the moon, as the curse would include all of the spell's power plus a little extra."

I looked around and all of the members of the group were still nodding thoughtfully.

"One problem," Half-Moon Spectacles finally said. "You're talking about Sarah now using not one type of blood magic, but two. And she's never even used her own type of magic before!" I couldn't help but glare in his direction; when pulling the blood magic from the moon had been his idea he seemed confident in my ability to perform such a "simple" bit of magic.

Gillan's response caught me by surprise at first. "I agree. It would be difficult. And it would still take the awareness of your own throsote, Sarah," he said, directing his comments at me. "It would be a long-shot," he continued, some of his enthusiasm fading, "but I think it should still be possible."

I nodded, caught by surprise again as Anders suddenly spoke. "It's too risky. You should just make the Hersotes mortal and not worry about the Slytons."

"If she values her life, I agree," spoke up Half-Moon Spectacles, and I actually sneered at him.

"I'm not letting you die. Nor your family," I said, hoping this would quell Anders' protests. "And I'm not staying indoors away from the blood moon and allowing all of the mortals to die at the hands of the Hersotes. I have to make this work." I stood as tall as possible and faced Gillan, whom I perceived as my greatest ally. "How should I start going about discovering my throsote?"

"Start in a quiet place, as throsotes are almost always natural things. Sometimes they're hereditary. You know the moon is two of your ancestors', so be sure to try that. And you said you thought your father's is water, so be sure to try that too. And wind, just in case that was your mother's throsote and not her magic like you guessed. Other than that, just experiment."

"And how do I experiment?" I asked.

"Just focus on it. Let yourself be free to move about it." I found his explanation far too vague, but if others had found their throsotes with such sorts of explanations, I hoped I could find mine too.

Chapter Twenty-Seven

"Are you sure you want me with you?" Anders asked as we stood on a high hill a couple of hours outside the city. Dark was falling rapidly, and the sparse trees in the area looked like imposing sentries on the smooth landscape. A river below gurgled loudly, its shiny black surface moving slightly in the starlight like a slithering snake.

"If they're going to be with me, you certainly can," I said, indicating our subtle, but not subtle enough pursuers with a backward nod of my head.

"Yea," Anders said, glancing back at the distant figures, obviously soldiers in their shiny armor. "I guess King Edward doesn't trust you to keep your word."

"He'll have me out in that moon one way or another," I said, looking up at the bright, mostly full moon above us. I took a deep breath. "Here we go." I stared into the moon, ran my eyes over its peculiar shadows. I raised my hands, as if in worship. I tried to imagine its rays coming down, bright and beautiful, filling my own body and existence.

But I found nothing. A normal light breeze, the same sounds of the river, and the occasional moo from a distant cow were all that rewarded my senses for my efforts.

"That was my main hope," I said, a bit forlornly.

"Throsotes aren't always passed down," Anders reminded me.

"I know. It's just with that being the throsote of two people related to me…. I'll try the river next."

And I did the same sorts of things, hoping that my father's throsote was passed down to me, and this search would be over with enough time to wrap my head around the real task at hand with the rapidly approaching blood moon. But nothing.

Although I had only tried two natural throsotes on this clear, cloudless night, I felt a disproportionate amount of despair. I needed this to be fast;

time was not a luxury I could afford if I were to save the lives of thousands of people. There was so much pressure, and somehow it had all landed on me.

I looked up at the sky, trying to blink back my tears. Beyond my water-filled eyes, the stars above me blurred together into a hazy explosion of lights. Something stirred, came to life inside of me, and I automatically lifted my hands. I blinked hard and the stars came into focus as my eyes cleared. All at once I felt a force, like a welcome, strong embrace, wrap around my arms and hands. I breathed in once, stared at the stars, their millions of twinkling lights above me, and I pushed out and away from myself. It had been the breeze wrapping around my limbs, and as I pushed forward, I pushed the breeze away, brushing the grass in its wild dance.

I took one last look at the stars and smiled. I then turned toward Anders, who stood a few feet to my side. In the starlight, I could see his peaceful smile, his dark eyes shining. "I knew you'd figure it out quickly."

I simply smiled in response and took his hand. We walked for the first hour in content silence, awkwardly passing the soldiers who had been following us, leaving them once again in our distant wake.

Eventually, as the buildings began to grow more numerous as we neared the capital, I spoke. "So you know it was the stars I was focusing on?"

"I thought so," Anders said.

"And that magic…. I'm fairly certain it was the breeze."

"That's what it looked like to me," he said, staring at me as we walked.

"I wonder if I have wind magic then, like I think my mother had."

"Did you want to try it out?" Anders asked, coming to a gentle halt.

"Eventually, I think. But for now, there's a different task I need to focus on. I don't want any distractions, any other knowledge of magic in my mind except for what I must do."

He nodded and continued walking, my hand still in his, warmed by his touch.

"Are you going to use a wand?"

"I might hold one, see if it feels natural," I said. "I think I'll ask that young man, Gillan. Certainly not the guy with the glasses."

"What an obnoxious man," Anders said, suddenly animated.

"I know!"

Our discussion then turned to our analysis of the royal advisers and their walled-in courtyard.

I went to bed that night full of hope. Looking out my window past the royal city walls, all looked peaceful and sleepy; an occasional light flickered out of tiny houses and the brilliant stars sparkled from above.

Chapter Twenty-Eight

The tea I held in my hands was bland, though it suited me well as the fragrant flowers around me created a pleasant sort of fog feeling. Raela and I sat together on reclined wooden chairs, a small tea table between us in the Lellios' courtyard. A new, simple wooden wand sat on the tea table too, having just received it from Gillan, whom I had just met there to discuss the use of a wand. He had recommended giving it a try, as it had helped him focus in his own beginner's pursuit of magic. Afterward, he had offered me the use of the courtyard for my own practice and relaxation. Ordering tea from one of the castle servants, I also requested Raela's presence were she available. And so the two had arrived almost simultaneously.

"I'm glad you could come have tea with me for a bit. I love the boys, but I woke up today really wanting some time with just us girls."

"I completely understand," she said, tucking a single strand of her sleek brown hair behind her ear, the rest of it held up in a perfect, tight bun. "I was really excited when I heard that you had some free time right now. Things here are...well...different."

"Yes. It's nice on paper, but at the same time....I guess it almost feels like a threatening environment. Prince Derrick seems honorable enough from the bit I've interacted with him, but his father is a different story."

"Mm," she agreed quietly, taking a sip of tea from the dainty white porcelain cup. After a minute of quiet while we intermittently blew on our hot tea and took tentative sips she said, "Not trying to put a damper on the day, but it is a bit strange to think that we are the only two women in the group now, I suppose. There's Celia's absence, of course. And I guess Agatha isn't truly part of us anymore either. Not after what she did."

I nodded my head in quiet contemplation. "I do hope that Agatha comes back around, though it's still difficult to wrap my head around not only her not coming with us, but of her informing the government of our plan, as if we were wanted criminals." I felt a bit of anger bubble up with my verbal acknowledgment of her betrayal. "If she hadn't have blabbed, perhaps we would not have been taken prisoner by those Hersotes back on Merendinappa Island."

"I know. I'm trying not to be angry at her, but it is a bit difficult," Raela added.

"Perhaps it was all Gregory's idea," I said, trying to direct my anger at someone other than our lifelong friend, though I guessed that directing it toward her soon-to-be husband would not yield much better results if I hoped to have Agatha as a friend again one day.

"Well, regardless, I'm really glad that I went with you," she said, and she smiled at me, her thin top lip disappearing entirely as she did so.

I smiled in response. "I'm glad you did too. And grateful. I don't know what I would have done without each of you by my side." I took another tiny sip of tea. Just then, the door to the courtyard burst open, and in my surprise I spilled a tiny splash of tea on the front of my lilac gown.

"Ladies, my apologies for this interruption," Orason said, his usually perfect poof of deep brown hair blown largely to the right in his apparent hurry. "James has just returned to the castle."

We at once stood and followed Orason back into the castle. Twisting and turning down several dark corridors, made darker by the bright sunlight in which we had just been sitting, we finally arrived at the throne room.

There, standing among a small group of soldiers before the king was James, his face tanned with red, sunburnt splotches on it, and his shirt as grimy as ours had been upon our arrival at the castle.

Upon seeing us, James ran toward us, first embracing Raela and then me. King Edward sat on his throne, his plump face scarlet and serious as he stared unabashedly at us.

"What's going on?" Raela asked James, her eyes darting back and forth from him to the soldiers still in the throne room to the king.

"I just finished telling the king," he said, leading the way out of the throne room. "We believe the Hersotes are on their way."

"On their way here?" I asked, fearful and partially unbelieving thanks to simple hope. "Are they coming for me?"

"Well, we believe they're coming for all of us," he said, wiping beaded sweat from his grimy brow. "We landed on Lystia farther north and made our way south, a group of Hersotes pursuing us for a short distance before they must have concluded you were not with us. Only a day from here, though, we ran into a Hersote woman, Geraldine. She warned us that the Hersotes are coming now. She said that she had spoken to you before, Sarah, in the prison?"

I nodded, and when I tried to swallow, my throat felt like sawdust.

"Well, she said she had told you before that they were building weapons and doing other things to prepare for a quick and effective attack. But with you leaving and the blood moon arriving, they're coming for you and to start the attack on all mortals now. She said they were hoping to have some other things to back them up, but with time and immortality on their side, they really have nothing to lose by coming now…and everything to lose if they wait with you free."

"So what's happening?" Raela asked, her voice a half-croak.

We were standing in the front greeting hall of the castle, Orason hovering awkwardly nearby while we chatted, presumably waiting to show James to a room.

"Well," James continued, licking his cracked lips, "the only thing we can do is fight them in the hope of delaying them until Sarah can…fix all of this." Although they had been looking at each other, they both turned toward me as James finished speaking, their expectant gazes upon me.

"I'll try my best," I said, and I walked quickly away, back toward the courtyard and my waiting wand.

Chapter Twenty-Nine

"Why don't you take a quick break?" Anders suggested calmly, squeezing my shoulders gently.

"Anders, the blood moon is in barely twenty-four hours, and the spies have said that the Hersotes should be here tomorrow afternoon. I have to practice my focus," I said, my knuckles standing out white as I grasped the light wood wand in the Lellios' courtyard.

"I know. But you've been practicing non-stop. You'll need rest too," he said.

"One more hour," I replied. He sighed and stood back and started singing a traditional folk song, quite off-key. His singing abilities being adequately average usually, I was unsure of whether the flat notes were due to his own exhaustion or an added element of distraction. Realizing that this train of thought had managed to distract me in and of itself, I focused my mind on a single pink flower among many. I pointed my wand at it and simply thought about it—what its satin-esque petals would feel like on my skin, the pale pink shade blocking out all other colors for me.

A tap on my shoulder brought me back to the courtyard in its entirety. "Okay. I've been singing for your distraction for at least fifteen more minutes. Let's stop for now, Sarah. You'll be fine. If you didn't even break into laughter at my ridiculous impersonation of Raela singing opera, I doubt concentration and focus will be an issue for you," he said with the hint of a smile.

"You were impersonating Raela?" I asked, having not caught an ounce of this even though he was presumably standing a foot away from me.

"My point exactly. Come on. Let's go eat something and get some sleep," he said, taking my hand. Truthfully exhausted, I finally allowed my legs to follow him.

Our whole group opted for a late dinner in Anders' room that night, seated on pillows and blankets on the floor. It was good to have James back, his brown hair smooth and clean now and his sunburn splotches looking much better and blended after a bath, despite his skin's deep pink hue. James had chosen a seat next to Raela and Anders had chosen one next to me. Thankfully, Darius didn't seem uncomfortable to be the only one not obviously paired up as he munched heartily on a large turkey leg.

The conversation was light throughout the meal, reminiscing of picnics back home and childhood squabbles, humorous now long after their brief fallouts and consequences.

Finally, wiping the last bit of food from my mouth, I said, "So, tomorrow night is the blood moon." Everyone stopped breathing as one. Barked orders could be heard out of the open window, carried on the warm summer air; the Lystian soldiers were preparing for battle. "What is everyone's plan for tomorrow?" I asked quietly.

"I'm fighting," James spoke up first, and all of our heads snapped toward him as if pulled on a leash.

"What?" Raela asked, her breathing increasing in rapidity.

"Leading a group of troops actually," he said, cutting at invisible food on his empty plate. "I—I know the Hersotes and the Lystians," he continued, looking up bravely then and making eye contact with each of us in turn. "The soldiers here like the way I think and strategize. I'm the one who sort of led them across the Lystian terrain up north while we were being pursued. I found caves and slopes where we could maintain an advantage if attacked. When they asked me to lead a group of men tomorrow, I accepted."

We all nodded our heads in reluctant agreement, even Raela. Darius was the first to speak. "Well, I for one would have never pictured timid James becoming the soldier out of our group, but it sounds like you're quite talented at it."

"Agreed," Anders added enthusiastically, and with Darius and Anders' uplifting declarations, I felt myself pulled back to the waterfall before we lived through the devastating earthquake, and the toasts that each of us delivered, our lives still happy and carefree.

"What are you doing tomorrow, Raela?" James asked somewhat guiltily, actually taking her hand in the first blatant show of attachment between the two of them.

"The royal singers asked me to join them in singing the Lystian anthem for the soldiers before the battle," she said, not withdrawing her eyes from James's.

"I'll be helping with equipment," Darius offered. "Seeing to necessary repairs and making sure that the supply wagons are continuously stocked. I offered my services to Marshall just this morning. He's the man who has been ordering my weapons for the military while we were still back in our village. Nice man, tiny little guy—not what I was picturing back home as the head of the military's equipment—but very knowledgeable."

We all nodded our heads in acknowledgment of Darius's role in the coming battle. "Well, that's a perfect role for you," I said.

"Speaking of which, I'll be right back," he said, and he jumped up, a few crumbs falling from his pants onto the floor. He raced out of the room, leaving the door ajar, and we could hear his own bedroom door open and close quickly before he reentered holding a small wooden box. Towering over me where I was seated on the floor, he held the box down to me. "For you."

As he sat back down, I opened the box and immediately began shedding tears at its content. "Thank you," I said quietly as I pulled out a wand. Bright silver and about the thickness of an average coin, it was much different than the sleek wooden one that had been given to me by Gillan. Still, this one was perfect for me; it contained tiny cutout bursts, like stars, opening to a hollow center.

"And wait, watch this," Darius said, gently taking the wand from me. He unscrewed the bottom which revealed a stubby candle attached to it. Looking around the darkening room as the sun continued to set outside, he stepped over to a candle and lit the one connected to the wand's open bottom. Lit, he screwed it back into the wand and handed it to me. All of the cutouts shone brightly like stars, a tiny version of my throsote in my hand.

All of us were in awe, transfixed by Darius's talent. "Thank you," I said most sincerely.

"You're welcome. If you don't want to use it, I completely understand. You need to do whatever you feel comfortable with obviously."

"No, no. I'll definitely be using this," I said, the wand still surprisingly cool in my hand despite the intense glow of the little stars. "It's perfect."

After a moment's continued reverence, Anders finally said, "Well, I guess I'm the only one without a helpful plan for tomorrow."

"I need you with me," I said at once, still holding my wand, and everyone's eyes went back and forth from me to Anders.

"You'll need your concentration," he said hesitantly. "And let's not forget what tomorrow night is for me," he said, and I could hear the fear and guilt in his voice. "I'm still not sure what kind of...reaction I'll have to the blood moon."

It was my turn to feel guilty, for in the midst of my worry and preparation, I had actually managed to briefly forget that tomorrow night would be one of uncertainty and worry for Anders as well.

"I was thinking," Anders hesitantly continued, "of asking to be locked in the prison cell under that hill. That way in case I grow especially violent or something, I'll be contained."

The sound of our collective breathing is all that filled the room for a minute, each of us lost in our own fears and thoughts.

"Then that's where I'll stand," I concluded.

"Wait. What? Where?" Anders asked, his dark eyes reflecting the bright candlelight around us as the rising moon's light washed us half in a natural light blue.

"On that hill. I might not be able to be underground with you, but at least we can be near each other," I explained. A thought then occurred to me, "Do you think that will be all right, James?"

He answered at once. "We expect the attack to come more from the open expanse to the north of the prison, so that should be fine, though obviously if the fighting moves more in that direction you'll have to change your plans. Both of you," he said, also glancing at Anders.

We nodded as a cool breeze blew into the room, extinguishing one of the candles near the window.

"I'll inform Captain Treash about your idea," James continued. "I suppose," he said, clearly thinking the next part through as he spoke, "that you should wait at one of the outlying cottages so you're close to that hill. That might be better anyway, as the Hersotes will be expecting you to be holed up in the castle."

"All right then," I said, and before each of us departed to our own rooms, Anders led our group in a desperate prayer. As he started praying, I kept my eyes open, soaking in the moon's pale light on my clasped hands. Picturing the light bright red suddenly, I closed my eyes too. Using my recent training, I pushed the image of the bloody light from my mind's eye, focusing on Anders' words of comfort. I would need to hold onto that comfort if I was ever going to focus enough to pull off what seemed highly improbable—using powerful magic to completely change the destiny of thousands of people.

That night, I dreamt of my mother, the same youthfulness in her face as there always was. I saw myself then too, my blonde hair now a darker shade than it had been in my childhood. I had her nose, I saw in my sleep as I compared the two of us, simply staring at each other—a small, feminine nose, though with the tiniest of bumps on its bridge. She was taller than I was, though, and so I still felt like a child next to her, though we both appeared of similar ages. Suddenly, my view of my mother was from within my own body again, through my own eyes. "Do I have wind magic like you, Mother?" I asked, my voice echoing as if in a cave, though the background was pure white around us.

She didn't speak, but shook her head.

"What then? Should I have learned it? I should have learned it. I feel so lost—so out of my depth!" I said.

She smiled patiently at my little outburst and then laid a hand on my shoulder. "Don't worry, Sarah," she whispered. "You have powerful magic."

She walked away, her pale blue dress blowing wildly around her in unfelt breeze. When I opened my eyes, the sun seemed high in the sky, though distorted. Throwing off my thin blanket, I sat upright, my bare feet hitting the smooth floorboards. Breathing shallowly, I walked to my window where I saw that the sun was hidden behind thin clouds. Panic seized me as I wondered what would happen if the moon were hidden that night. Just then, the sun came out from one of the numerous clouds in the sky, temporarily obliterating my fear.

Turning back into my room, I pulled my nightgown off over my head and put on the dress I had chosen the night before and laid out on a chair. Perhaps in a morbid state of mind I had chosen it, though I still felt confident in my choice this morning: a tight blood red bodice and skirt with a thick, white satin sash. Putting it on, the clasps in the front were uncomfortable, but I continued to fasten them.

Standing in front of the mirror in my room, the bright red of the dress was shocking against my blonde hair, bringing only my blushing cheeks into sharp focus against my blue eyes, blonde hair, and abnormally pale skin.

Surveying my appearance, the memory of my mother rushed into me once more, though it was her horrible death that besieged me at this time. I could see the blood spatters from the moon soaking into her off-white dress. If I failed, the moon's blood spatters would not be visible to anyone in my bright red dress, and I found this thought oddly comforting, however morbid.

Life of blood Meraldia's spell had stated. And it was true—I indeed was destined to have a life of blood. But still, perhaps I could use that blood to not only my benefit, but the benefit of many, many others. Choosing to embrace this life this day, I took a deep breath despite my tight dress and stepped out into the castle hallway, a bright scarlet ghost against the dark gray stone.

Chapter Thirty

The cottage was stifling. I sat at the small kitchen table with Anders, holding hands, but not speaking, as ten soldiers stood around us, uncomfortably crammed into the room that had been offered us by the cottage's frightened residents. Despite their natural discomfort at the sudden appearance of Lystian guards, the couple who lived there had been extremely gracious about offering us the temporary use of their home when we explained our need for a place to stay close by the prison. Only a ten minute walk away, we had remained crammed in the cottage all afternoon while the wife prepared us all a meal, a vegetable soup, and her husband stayed out of our way in their bedroom.

Late afternoon was upon us now, and I could sense the movements of unease and the desire for real motion by the soldiers around us. "Should we go?" I eventually asked after catching the eye of one of the soldiers. At my words, several of the guards noticeably relaxed, clearly excited to be on the move.

"That's fine," the soldier whom I had made eye contact with replied. And standing, we all made a hasty exit with muttered thanks to the woman whose home we had used.

The walk to the prison was all uphill. We had heard the beginning of fighting less than an hour before. The Lystian army's goal was cautious stalling of the Hersotes. The longer the Lystians could simply hamper the Hersotes' progress and stay alive, the better their chances. Nevertheless, I could make out the distant cries of war in the background and the loud cracks and rumblings of catapults. As the sun quickly set, I began to see unearthly bursts of light from beyond the hill which we climbed. Presumably the Hersotes with magic suited to warriors led this charge, and I guessed the flashes of lights I was seeing were due to the use of such magic. I squeezed Anders' hand, hoping that by the time I was able to use the blood moon, it would not be too late for the brave soldiers of Lystia.

Climbing nearly to the top of the hill, I made sure to stay just out of sight of the battle in front of and below us. I did not want to be visible to the Hersotes, but I also did not want to be further distracted by what I only assumed was a grisly scene indeed. Coming to a stop, the soldiers silently created a semi-circle behind me, their swords out and to their sides.

Looking at Anders, I saw that his brow was creased in near-agony. "You'll be fine," he said, leaning down to give me a brief kiss before I could say anything. "I love you. I need to go now, though. I've already waited far too long," he said. He nodded quickly at one of the soldiers and raced into the cellar-like door to the prison.

I stared after him longingly, wishing he could stay above with me. The soldier returned in a minute, shutting the main door to the prison behind him. "He's fine," he said to me. "Reluctant to go in the cell, but he went." The soldier half turned away from me before adding, "If that's the beginning of his worst self, it seems you chose an admirable man indeed." I actually smiled as the soldier resumed his position in the semi-circle behind me.

The clouds from earlier that day had completely dissipated, and the moon was rising quickly, in front of me and to the right, slightly beyond the castle. It was pure white in its radiance, and part of me doubted that it could ever change to something so ghastly.

The darkness around me grew as the comforting stars shined brighter and the full moon steadily climbed the sky. Perhaps an hour passed, and the groanings of war invaded my mind.

There was only a very faint breeze, and so I turned around and requested the fire starter from the guards. One came forward and handed it to me. Almost ceremoniously, I unscrewed the bottom of my wand and lit the new candle that had been placed there. Placing the candle back within my wand, the little metal stars danced brightly. I gazed at the full moon, gaining height now. I took deep breaths, slowing my heartrate, focusing my mind.

And all of a sudden, the moon went dark. I breathed all the deeper. I had to focus. I had to be calm. And then, faintly at first, but growing in intensity each second, the moon reappeared, a pale red. As I watched, it seemed that the moon's craters slowly filled with blood, trickling over then to the rest of the moon's surface, flooding higher and higher.

And I could hear Meraldia's voice loud and clear:

Blood of mine
Life of blood
It drips to you
Mistakes undone
Call the power of your blood
Send to every corner
Death for those who wait forever

I was that little girl back on the top of Merendinappa Island. Alone and scared. I forced myself to be present, focusing oddly on the battle sounds down below. Brief thoughts of my friends flickered through my mind, resting on Anders, wishing he could be with me. I thought the top of the moon looked as if it might be beginning to melt downward. The time was approaching.

And that's when I heard a horrible crash and clang of metal. I barely had time to process that it came from within the prison when the door in the hill burst open and Anders shot out of it, his eyes dark yet blazing. Running at me full speed, he tackled me hard, knocking the wind from my lungs as his knee slammed into my gut. His hair was sticking up in odd places, as if he had just awoken from a fitful night's sleep, and there were deep creases around his eyes and a grimace on his mouth.

It seemed darker to me up on that hillside for a moment, and in my hazy mind I detachedly noticed that the fire from my candle wand had been extinguished when Anders grabbed me, though I still held the wand tight in my uncompromisingly firm grip.

Anders spoke then, his voice harsh and barely recognizable as his own. "Come at me with those swords, and you will all die." My eyes remained focused on Anders' face, only inches in front of mine, though he was staring at the soldiers around us. "There is a door to hell right to my right. Take one more step toward me, and I'll throw Sarah into it. She will never be able to come out, and you all will die. So…stay right where you are." His words were each punctuated cruelly. The blood moon was blocked from sight by his face, his lips parted in a sort of sneer, an unheard growl present. The soldiers must have stopped their approach, for he looked at me then, his pupils taking up the entirety of his eyes, looking almost through me instead of at me.

"What are you doing, Anders?" I whispered at him. And for just a moment, his eyes truly focused on mine.

"You can't do this. I don't believe you can do this," he said, still resting on each word as he spoke.

I swallowed a lump in my throat. "You have to let me try."

"No. I don't," he said harshly. Then, very quietly, "I'm going to bring you back into the prison with me. Underground, away from the blood moon, the curse can't take hold." But despite his words, he didn't move a muscle.

"But our friends. My father. So many people will die."

"But we'll still be alive."

"Anders, if the Hersotes win, we might be alive, but most likely spending our eternity in a prison, without sunlight."

"We don't need sunlight," he said with an animalistic snarl.

"Anders, you have to let me try," I pleaded.

Once again, his eyes truly focused on mine as he whispered, "I can't."

His strength pushing me down against the ground was nearly rib shattering, and with a sickening feeling in my stomach I realized that he must have literally broken out of the prison cell somehow; the blood moon was clearly having a horrible effect on him, and I knew that there were probably many different levels to not only his determination, but his admission of "I can't."

"But you need to. Or everything we've fought for will be lost," I whispered to him.

His head snapped up as he glared in the direction of a soldier who must have made a movement. Satisfied once more, Anders turned to look at me again, his eyes not focused on anything. All on the hill was quiet as the sounds of death filled the background of the night. Then, so quiet I could barely hear him. "Kill me."

My response was immediate and vehement. "I can't."

"You need to," he said, his body unmoving and strong on top of mine. "I can't keep fighting the urge to hide you from the moon."

The horror of my choice was upon me—kill Anders and try to save everyone else, or let Anders live, allowing him to most likely drag me to the underground prison, doomed to spend eternity hiding from the wretched Hersotes after they've killed our friends and the other mortals.

Nevertheless, the thought of killing Anders was incomprehensible. I would hate myself forever.

But if I allowed him to live, he would hate himself forever.

My wand still tight in my hand, I glanced upward and beyond Anders, catching sight of a star. I would need to use the blood moon's curse, directed at Anders, but direct sight of the blood moon was still blocked by him, his face only an inch from mine. I instead focused on that bright star visible to me. And as tears began to fill my eyes, all I could think was, I need to take Anders' life. My stomach tightened at the thought, but I repeated it to myself, completely nauseated and filled with self-loathing.

As tears threatened to blur the star above me, I thought one more time, I need to take Anders' life. And all at once, there was a blinding burst of light as my wand reignited and Anders collapsed on top of me.

With an instinctive, repulsed feeling and a desire to crawl out of my own body, I pushed his body from mine. He rolled lifelessly and limply from me, and I jumped to my feet with a half-sob, half-retching sound.

My bright wand in my hand, I looked at the moon in a state of frenzy. The moon was pure white again, but I could see the blood far off, heavy droplets coming down from the sky.

For a moment, my mind was completely blank. Shaking uncontrollably then, I held my wand up, dazzling and hot against my hand. Shocking me back to reality, I looked at the droplets of blood, seemingly right before me even though they were still high up in the sky. I looked through my wand, through the stars, and to the wretched curse.

I pictured Margaret, a typical Hersote in her appearance with her unusually husky voice. I could hear it—hear it jeering at Anders and me in our jail cell. And I reached with her hand and withdrew her power from the curse.

It was clear to me. The bright red of the falling blood became a shade darker, not as bright, not as threatening. And then I turned inward once more and thought of my other relative—the intense Meraldia. Pale and almost angel-like in appearance, washed in the candlelight of her cell. And yet there was a harshness to her, and it was this harshness that I could feel growing closer, ready to rain down on us. And channeling all of my thoughts through Meraldia, I changed her curse. The cycle will not cease immediately. It will make us—all of us immortals—mortal once more. We will pick up where our bodies left off.

The blood rain grew closer and closer and closer. Looking up, it splattered across my face and arms and against my clothes. I closed my eyes. My limbs felt suddenly heavy, and I dropped to my knees. Pain shot through my body.

And yet I didn't die.

I closed my eyes and rested my head on the cool grass, huddled into myself. And then I heard the yells from beyond the hill grow in triumphant intensity, and I knew it had worked. I was mortal. We were all mortal.

I opened my eyes, placed my shining wand on the ground to my side, and crawled on my hands and knees toward Anders.

Facing the sky peacefully, his eyes were closed as if he were sleeping, his black hair falling messily across his forehead.

He wasn't sleeping, though.

I dropped my head onto his unmoving chest and sobbed, kicking at the ground weakly with one of my feet.

The soldiers around me shifted slightly, but I did not spare a glance for them.

Reflected on Anders' cold body, I could see the pale light of the moon very slowly sink, and the warm soft glow of the orange rising sun begin to simmer from beyond the horizon.

I finally felt a hand on my shoulder then, and for one insane moment I thought it was Anders' hand. Instead, I turned to look into the concerned face of Gillan.

"I don't even know how—but I had to. The blood moon," I whimpered, the roar of the battle still overwhelming in the distance.

His eyes were soft and sympathetic despite the downward slant of his eyebrows. His features then softened entirely as he glanced backward at the ground. "Your wand," he simply said, staring at the glowing metal rod, brighter than the sun that still had not yet poked out of the earth.

I crawled the few feet back to it, my body aching all over as I did so. Picking it up, it seemed to pulse oddly in my hand. I crawled back over to Anders, and with some innate knowledge, gently touched the tip of my wand to his chest as I leaned over, brushed the hair back from his forehead, and kissed him.

The breath I felt was not merely my own reflected back. My wand instantly cooled in my hand. "Anders?" I whispered, hopeful against commonsense.

"Sarah?" he responded, and I threw myself against his chest once more, sobbing with relief.

Chapter Thirty-One

My type of magic was called Containment, apparently an extremely rare type. Thankfully, Gillan had witnessed the end of my unintentional show of magic or I would have had a near impossible time explaining Anders' obvious death and then unbelievable breath of life hours later.

"The last known user of Containment magic died almost fifty years ago, according to our records," Gillan told me in the castle courtyard later that day. "It's extremely rare, and can be extraordinarily powerful. I've never seen it used until this morning."

And indeed it was very unique. It seemed that I had the power to harness something, whether around my body or in a physical object. I could then release it when I wished. So, the night that I had found my throsote, I was not so much creating or stirring the wind as I was simply drawing it in and then releasing it.

And then the night of the battle, I looked at my throsote and took Anders' life—quite literally. I took it and contained it in my hollowed-out wand, releasing it back into his body just as the brilliant sun broke over the horizon.

My preoccupation with Anders seemed to wash out all other details for the first part of that next day. Curious for answers, I finally allowed myself to be diverted around noon when I went to meet Gillan in the courtyard. Anders had come with me, for we had other questions we wanted answered by that point.

"So, we're not dead," I pointed out quite obviously once he had finished explaining Containment. "Are we mortal?"

"I believe so," Gillan said with a smile. "And I think that Anders is as well, since his life, though not in his body, was on this earth. We can perform a little test, though."

Gillan pulled a tiny knife from within his shirt pocket and indicated that he wanted Anders' hand. Warily, Anders extended his arm, and Gillan made the tiniest of pricks on his finger.

"Ouch!" Anders exclaimed as a tiny trickle of blood came forth. His cheeks quickly matched the red of his blood. "Sorry. I just wasn't expecting it to feel like that," he said sheepishly.

I already knew that I was mortal—I was more aware of my beating heart and my greedy lungs. My body was fatigued in a way once unknown to me; I had never realized how much being immortal shielded me from basic bodily feelings. What I had at first mistaken for pain, I was beginning to realize, was my body simply demanding the rest I had so reluctantly provided it within the recent past.

And with all of these realizations, I still felt myself put out my own hand for Gillan, who raised his eyebrows in question, but pricked my finger nonetheless. I let out my own little exclamation of pain and then watched the tiny trickle of blood as if in a trance. I supposed I had blood of my own while immortal, but I never saw it; wounds healed almost instantaneously before. It was warm feeling on my finger and throbbed with the beating of my heart ever so slightly. On a strange impulse, I popped the bloody finger into my mouth, immediately regretting this action as it tasted like I was sucking on a piece of metal. "Yuck," I simply said in response to Anders' quizzical stare, my face drawn up in a grimace.

Meanwhile, Gillan was surveying our faces curiously, a small smile playing on his lips. "It's like watching an adult be born," he finally said, a bit in awe. Breaking our mesmerized glances and stares, Gillan finally declared, "I'll bet you're hungry. Let's have some lunch and see if your friends have returned yet."

Darius joined us almost immediately for lunch, cleaned up but dark circles under his tired eyes from a night full of arming and rearming soldiers, hearing the screams of battle so nearby. And then, as our plates were being cleared, Raela entered the dining room where we also sat by that point with Gillan and the other Lellio advisers.

"Raela! Where have you been?" I exclaimed, jumping up and giving her a hug when I saw her.

"Waiting for James," she said, and her smile despite her slumping posture answered the question before she spoke. "He's all right."

Anders and Darius gave sighs of relief behind me.

"Wonderful," I said. "Not injured?"

"Just some cuts and bruises. Nothing major," she said. "He's cleaning himself up now. He didn't give me the details yet, but he said the battle was intense."

I had not doubted this for a second.

Details of the battle quickly came back to us, through James and others. The Hersotes who had been leading the attack had had fire magic, wind magic, and the magic of disorientation. Using all of these distractions, some Hersotes had followed up with simple bows and arrows. Meanwhile, the Lystian army had depended largely on objects and maneuvers to impede the Hersotes' progress. Catapults had been used to try to slow down the enemy; even if being hit with one wouldn't kill them, it would at least give them pause as they had to stand up once more or free themselves from being held to the ground in a best case scenario. James's soldiers had spent time digging ditches and creating barriers with spears and other things that were not easily passed. Others had spent time deploying and preparing nets, both with weighted ends sent from a catapult as a deterrent and also up close with the idea of actually capturing Hersotes and thus taking them out of the battle. Some were captured more easily than others; the hearts of some were simply not in the fight from the first, while others did not have the magic to free themselves.

Gathered in my room the night after the battle, James's bumps and bruises had all been cleaned and bandaged with the exception of a quite noticeable black eye. "A Hersote nearby used wind magic," he explained. "Sent a rock right at my face. Fortunately, my vision seems fine now."

While James's account of the battle compared to other accounts that had reached us, I found his description of the blood moon to be the most haunting. "When the moon turned red and started to bleed downward, the fighting grew especially intense. The screams of the Hersotes became louder and their magic seemed more powerful in their fear. The whole battlefield seemed to light up from the fire magic then. I mean, you need to assume that they thought they were all about to die, not become mortal, especially with the blood dripping from the moon. As the moon grew white again, I lost track of the blood that was raining down. It didn't touch me at all. And it was at this point that the fighting seemed to stop for a brief second. A Hersote was near me, though I was hidden behind some rocks pretty well and she didn't see me there. She had been one of the ones using a bow and arrow, but she stopped completely for perhaps a minute, just looking at her limbs unbelievingly, hanging onto her bow with one limp arm. Then she looked up just as an arrow pierced her chest. She fell immediately, lifted her head to look at the arrow, and then it dropped backward. I—I know she was fighting against us, but I kind of had to feel bad for her. She was so confused, and then it was just all over."

I stared into my lap as he talked, goosebumps popping up on my arms in the cool night air. I felt Anders wrap a comforting arm around me as James continued, "Some of the Hersotes began screaming in fear. Knowing that it had worked then, the group I was with all breathed a huge sigh of relief, though we still had to make it off the battlefield alive. Some of the Hersotes surrendered right away, tearing off pieces of clothing, making impromptu white flags and approaching us cautiously from the side. Others initiated an immediate retreat, while a surprisingly large group kept fighting anyway. Either they hadn't realized what was going on in their own excitement, or they had reached a point where they didn't care. Eventually, though, we were able to subdue all of them, their magical powers notwithstanding."

"So the Hersotes are kind of like the Lellios now?" Darius asked. "Mortal magic users?"

"I think so," I took the liberty of answering.

"And the Slytons?" Darius asked.

"Mortals like you," I answered again, though Anders touched my arm gently with his free hand to stop me.

"Actually, not quite," he said. "Mortal, yes. But...well," he squirmed where he sat next to me on the floor. "Let's just say, before Raela came with the news that James was alive and well, I could hear both of your fears that he had died," he said, looking at me and Darius.

I quickly took in breath. "I'm so sorry," I said, feeling oddly guilty.

"No need to be sorry," Anders said.

"It's just...I know it's not always bad to hear people's fears, but I was hoping you would be rid of all of those powers since you...well, you thought they were rather evil?"

"I used to," he said reassuringly. "But we've seen some good come from them. And now that I have the ability to die...well, I do hope I would not still wind up in hell."

"Of course you wouldn't," I said at once.

He smiled at me gratefully. "Well, I apologize in advance if I'm still unbearable during full moons too."

"I'll just lock you in a closet," I said, half-jokingly. And it was then that I realized we were discussing me being around him during future full moons. The realization wasn't shocking, though; of course I would be with him.

Anders must have realized the same thing, for he said, "Well, I'm hoping that you'll be able to lock me in our closet."

"Is this a marriage proposal, because I'd say that was the worst line ever," Darius half-whispered jokingly.

Anders laughed and his pale cheeks turned scarlet. "Agreed," he said. "Let me try again. Sarah," he said, moving his body to face me directly, "will you marry me?"

I couldn't help but emit a tiny laugh as I heard Raela's girly gasp while I looked in Anders' dark eyes, hopeful. "Of course," I said, and Anders leaned in and kissed me right there.

Pulling back happily, he reached into his pocket and withdrew a tiny ring, a bright red ruby sitting in yellow gold. "For our engagement," he said happily, and I held it against my lap, staring at it in awe where it stood out against my fresh cream dress that day. As it glistened there, I was reminded momentarily of blood. I found that the thought of blood no longer repulsed me as it had, though. After all, I was simply thankful that it coursed through Anders and my veins, for we were happy, healthy, and still able to look forward to a long life together surrounded by friends and family.

Epilogue

We stayed at the castle for two weeks following the blood moon. Gillan tutored me on beginning to explore my Containment magic, and I found that I was able to hold wind in my hands and store the scent of roses in a jar. One of the other advisers begged me to take his life briefly just to try it out, but I declined; taking someone's life once had been unbearable enough.

At the end of our stay, the advisers had actually offered me a position as a Royal Adviser. Although not flat-out declining, I told them that I would have to give the offer some time to consider while I really practiced my new magic type. Although rare and obviously powerful after my inadvertent demonstration of it with Anders' life, I would have felt like an imposter to accept so coveted a position after using my magic only a handful of times with no idea yet as to its limits. Plus, Anders and I missed our families and village and were eager to head back home and begin a new life there.

James, meanwhile, had been offered a position as a captain and chief strategist for Lystia's military. Apparently, his mind for wartime strategy had continued to impress during the Battle of the Blood Moon, as it was already being referred to. James had excitedly accepted the position, while Raela had also reaccepted a position in the capital as one of the royal singers. Still, they traveled back to the village with us and Darius, as Anders and I planned to have our wedding a couple of weeks after our arrival.

While still in Harpson, we had each sent word to our parents, assuring them of our health and safety. And then following the battle, word of the events had spread rapidly across the country, seemingly carried on the wind. So our arrival back home was met with much excitement and fanfare. People who had shut me and Anders out for being immortal when we left, shook our hands with enthusiasm. It was strange and hypocritical, but I was still relieved by the hospitable return.

The Stones had been overjoyed to see us and tell us of their relief in shedding their immortality. "It's just—it's been so tiring, living for so many years, constantly fighting off all of our Slyton urges. We were at least blessed to find another immortal to be with," Anders' mom said tearfully. "Plus, there's something almost romantic about aging with the person you love," she said.

"Speaking of which," Anders began proudly, announcing our engagement to his ecstatic family.

My father had also been extremely excited about Anders and my engagement, and relieved that though not immortal, I was happy. "It's just strange, though. I've never had to worry about you becoming hurt. Well…," he quickly amended as we had just finished telling him the complete tale of our adventures, "perhaps I should have been a little worried. An eternity in that jail cell in Grotania—I can't even fathom." While I had no desire to ever return to Grotania, we received news of it from Prince Derrick shortly upon our return to our village. The Lystian army had taken control of Grotania, and were dealing with the registration and determination of the various Hersotes there who had either remained during the time of the battle or who had fled there following it. He assured me that they were handling the process with as much kindness as they could, not desiring to unnecessarily imprison any Hersotes who simply wished to live out the rest of their days in peace. They had been jailing Hersotes who still posed an active threat, though some, like my great-great-grandmother, Meraldia, had killed themselves on discovering their new mortality.

After this bit of information arrived, though, I heard nothing more from the capital leading up to my wedding day, and I was glad of it. We had all had so much going on, that it was quite refreshing to only have to think about designing my wedding dress, which I decided to make myself, as opposed to focusing on throsotes and escaping an inescapable underground jail.

We were catapulted into action two days before my wedding, however, with the arrival of another full moon. "It's all right," Anders assured me as I met him at his house early that evening to lock the Stones in their rooms. "I'm used to this." I did not like that he still had to endure that period of anger, but after our adventures, he assured me that there were worse things he could have to deal with, and I was inclined to agree.

When our wedding day arrived, Raela, my maid of honor, helped me dress in my bedroom. "You look stunning," she said. "Like an angel." The sun had just set, and the waning moon was already bright in the sky.

I smoothed the fabric of my gauzy white dress, puffy and flowing. Anders and I were to be married on a hill nearby on this clear night, where we had once enjoyed many picnics with our friends.

We were about to leave for the hill when there was a knock on my door and we were surprised to see Darius and James there, dressed in fine dark clothing. "So sorry, but Anders is in your barn, and would like a word before you leave."

"He's not supposed to see her in her dress before the wedding!" Raela protested.

"It's fine," I said calmly, more curious as to what Anders could want out in my barn.

The others waited in my house while I walked out to the plain, tiny barn. Stepping inside, I saw that he had lit a single candle and was idly petting my father's donkey. His black hair was just as adorably mop-like as always, and his blemish-free skin was almost reflective in the candlelight, with the exception of his cheeks, full of life and color. He had on black pants and a white dress shirt, stiff and somewhat regal in appearance.

Turning toward me in the dim candlelight, his eyebrows rose at the sight of me, his deep brown eyes shining excitedly. "You look beautiful."

"Thank you," I said, almost bashfully. "You look handsome as always." I took a deep, though playful breath. "So…what are we doing standing here with Burrows?" I asked, indicating the donkey.

Anders smiled at me, though the smile quickly disappeared. "It's just, before we do this, I want to be certain that you're absolutely sure you wish to marry me."

"Of course," I said, thrown off. "Why wouldn't I be?"

"Well, you know I can still hear your fears when you have them. I don't want you to always be uncomfortable around me."
I actually laughed slightly. "I'm just glad that you seem to listen."

He smiled briefly. "And you'll actually have to still lock me in a room I guess on the nights of full moons."

"I can live with that," I said seriously.

"All right. Well then there's just…." And with a heave of his chest, his words tumbled out, "The night of the blood moon I actually attacked you! I tried to stop you completely—didn't believe in you at all! I just don't know that I could marry me if I were you. Not after that."

"Anders, it was the blood moon."

"Yes, it was the blood moon, but it was still me in the blood moon. Instead of fighting with James or doing anything useful, I actually put you in danger."

I went over to him and touched his arm gently, locking my eyes on his. "Anders, it's all right. It was the blood moon's effect on you, not you. And plus you're forgetting. You went to hell and came back for me."

He brushed off these last words with a half-snort.

"I'm serious," I said, and my almost stern words demanded his eye contact once more. "You saved me and put your own eternal happiness at risk. And aside from that specific instance, you've always been there, supporting me. Even when we were just friends, you were always there for me, even if being there for me was giving me my space since I was afraid of you knowing my fears. You've been wonderful, Anders. I love you, and nothing that happened the night of the blood moon has changed that or ever will."

He nodded his head, taking both of my hands in his.

"All right then," he said, taking a deep, cleansing breath. "In that case…I'll meet you on the hill in a bit." The trace of a smile returned to him as he leaned down and kissed my cheek before walking with purpose out of the hay-strewn barn. I waited a minute to give him a head start and then walked back into the house, finding an anxiously-waiting Raela still in my room.

"There you are! Is everything all right?" she demanded.

"Yes," I said happily.

"The boys just left, so we can probably leave too if we take our time," she said.

"All right," I agreed, and we walked through my childhood home, out into the night. My dress seemed to glow with the moon as we walked.

The hill was only a few minutes away, and I could see the assembled people there, each holding a candle.

Anders was already standing at the front, Darius and James standing nearby.

"Are you ready for this?" Raela asked excitedly.

"Yes," I said, my eyes not breaking from Anders, and even at this distance it seemed that he was returning my gaze.

As we started to ascend the rolling hill, a light breeze rushed past, carrying the scent of honeysuckles. On an impulse, I reached out my empty hands and grabbed some of it. I could feel the swirling breeze there in front of me, oddly free despite me keeping it there. Then, as I reached the edge of the people gathered for the wedding, I released it. It playfully swirled around our guests up to Anders, pushing at his hair and putting a smile on his serious face. I inhaled the honeysuckles once more, and, with my eyes still not moving from Anders, walked forward, my beating heart joyful and at peace.

ABOUT THE AUTHOR

Ellen Parry Lewis is the author of the young adult novels *Risking a Life*, *Avenging Her Father*, *An Unremarkable Girl*, and *Future Vision*. Before turning to fiction full-time, Ellen was a freelance reporter for several newspapers. Ellen lives in New Jersey with her husband, daughter, son, and two dachshunds.

OTHER BOOKS BY ELLEN PARRY LEWIS

Future Vision

Samantha Bell is an ambitious high school student with a bright future until one fateful night at the local fair. She decides to go through the controversial Future Vision exhibit. This attraction allows viewers to see up to twenty seconds of their personal future. Because of the possible risks, viewers must ingest a dissolvable pill immediately afterward, causing them to forget what they had just witnessed. Samantha tries to take the future into her own hands, though, when she smuggles a pen inside the attraction. Although she was forced to forget what she had seen, she leaves the attraction with an ominous feeling and three mysterious words written on her hand: Snow, fight, and ca. Samantha feels she must figure out what those three words mean before the event occurs and possibly ruins her life.

An Unremarkable Girl

Krisanna Wether happily lived in a peaceful farming village until it was raided and her people were enslaved by a neighboring kingdom. She finds herself in a dangerous situation where she is mistaken for a traveling princess. While living under this false identity, Krisanna meets a handsome, kind enemy soldier who makes her question her hatred towards her captors. Her feelings toward him blossom, enveloping him in her dangerous web of deceit.

Krisanna's efforts to free her family and people take this once seemingly unremarkable farm girl on a journey as a prisoner, a princess, a fugitive, a foreigner, a member of nobility, and more. She soon discovers that in order to save her people and the man she has grown to love, she will have to make difficult decisions that challenge her definitions of good and evil.

Avenging Her Father

A strange twist of fate allows the lovely Laersona Wylos to narrowly escape death in the ethnic cleansing of the Peretians ordered by the cruel King Laurenso. Her father was not as fortunate and was brutally murdered by the king's men. Heartbroken and alone, Laersona vows to avenge him and her people by destroying the man who ordered their demise. Her thirst for royal blood takes her on a dangerous journey to the castle where she meets the king's dashing young prince and learns shocking royal secrets. Will her growing feelings for the prince distract her from her true purpose and how will he react when he discovers her quest for revenge?

Risking a Life

Constantly surrounded by luxury, but unable to partake in it, eighteen-year-old maid Louisa West is unsatisfied with her life. On New Year's Eve 1854, though, she gains knowledge that will change her life forever. A man tells her of a demon in the woods—a demon who offers wagers resulting in either unfathomable fortune or irreversible loss. If the person wins, they gain a promised reward. If they lose, the cost is the life of another person. Finding that she can no longer take her current circumstances, Louisa desperately seeks out the mysterious demon. She gambles the life of a fellow servant to find romance with the dashing and wealthy William Knight. As time unfolds, Louisa realizes that she has made a terrible mistake—one that could lead to death and lost love.